GATOR GLADES

JOHN LEE SCHNEIDER

SEVERED PRESS
HOBART TASMANIA

GATOR GLADES

"I'm not big on the conservation of crocodiles. They're evil bastards... See, they're not unpredictable... they're the one big predator that, if it's big enough, and you're available enough, it's going to go for you every single time."

Quinton 'Crocodile' Marvin

CHAPTER 1

The swamp was always watching you.

Wherever you looked out on the water, a thousand eyes blinked back, from under every log, behind every leaf – all the lush, primitive life that grew out of the sultry primeval soup – much of it dangerous, almost all of it predatory.

The eyes that watched were hungry, with appetites that did not discriminate. People lost on the water were rarely found. The swamp left no trace.

Alex had lived on the Everglades all his life, and had grown up with its alligators, copperheads and water-moccasins, its diamondback rattlers and assortment of stinging insects.

Venomous, carnivorous, deadly dangers of all kinds. You almost got used to it – no different than watching for the dangers of car-traffic.

But in recent years, things had changed.

Alex had seen it from the front-lines – he worked at 'Gator Glades', the largest reptile park in Florida, and probably in the entire western hemisphere. It bordered on the coast, right at the edge of Everglades National Park. Alex had been head of maintenance for nearly ten years.

The Everglades themselves were in a time of ecological crisis. For decades, the degradation of the local ecosystem had been held at bay by conservation efforts, but just in the last few years, Alex had begun to believe the cause might finally have been lost.

Part of it was destruction of the habitat itself. City zoning projects had managed to drain large portions of the swamp right into local neighborhoods – homeowners were suddenly finding alligators in their pools and front porches, or even in their kitchens.

It might have started with human encroachment, but it wasn't long before the swamp encroached back.

But even worse was the widespread proliferation of invasive species. The Everglades' indigenous fauna was under relentless assault by any number of foreign invaders, from Nile monitors and tegu lizards, to wild pigs, which all flourished in the swampy environment, and were pushing local endangered species to the brink of extinction.

Currently, Gator Glades was involved in an invasive species removal project. For decades, the Everglades had seen an influx of exotics from a variety of sources. The black market worked out of Florida like a weigh-station, but the legal trade proved even worse.

For one thing, because of the proximity to an ostensibly natural habitat, people had a tendency to release their exotic pets into the wild – a not-inconsiderable problem. Unlike the semi-legendary cases of baby gators being flushed down toilets in New York City and surviving in the sewers – a barely-livable environment – the Glades were a virtual paradise.

Things really went south in 1992 when Hurricane Andrew blew over the storage warehouse where the incoming shipments of exotic animals were stationed, releasing large numbers of both sexes into the surrounding swamp – snakes, lizards, insects, spiders – alien-species from all over the world – an industrial-scale invasion.

Among the more worrisome exotics, were breeding populations of cobras, including king cobras, as well as their deadly cousins the mambas – a garden worker was bitten and nearly killed by a green mamba while working on a property just along the border of the Everglades.

Pythons, in particular, had taken root – predominantly the large, although relatively mild-tempered Burmese python. But nasty, aggressive African rock pythons were establishing a presence as well – and even more problematically, the giant reticulated python – the one big constrictor commonly known to actually *eat* its human victims.

Gator Glades had a big retic on-site – a twenty-five foot, three-hundred pound female called Buffy – one of the largest in captivity – and you could see the predatory gleam in its eyes as it stared back at you through the glass of its cage – like it was happy to see you... but not in a good way.

And they were out there in the swamp right now – living, growing, and reproducing. Python eggs had been found mere yards away from people's houses.

But beyond the simple fact of them *being* there, there was also the issue of all those different, closely-related species living among each other, and potentially hybridizing.

A documented phenomenon called 'hybrid vigor' is known to produce abnormally LARGE first-generation offspring, and there had been some speculation among experts of what might be produced should dangerous invasive species like Burmese and rock pythons, or God forbid, retics, start interbreeding.

And while that was a nightmarish thought when dealing with three-hundred pound serpents, it was quite another when you were talking about two-thousand pound crocodiles.

Gator Glades' attractions were reptilian in general, with snakes and lizards of all kinds – they had a number of Komodo dragons, a scary critter all on its own – and of course, alligators – although putting gators in a zoo in Florida was a lot like charging admission to see raccoons and possums.

Their real specialty was crocodiles.

Alex was working at the croc-pond today, fixing a drainage pump. And he could see them out there now, at least a hundred and fifty animals, their beady, ever-observant eyes poking up just above the waterline, unblinking and single-minded – watching you – happy to see you.

But not in a good way.

The park supervisor had sent him over that morning – a tough-minded, albeit easy-on-the-eyes, forty-something woman named Jen Summers, who Alex had seen wrestle a ten-foot 'gator off a golf-course and into a park-department truck single-handed – and she had given Alex the same, stern no-nonsense warning about the croc-pond that she did every day without fail.

"Don't you ever get near the water," she told him.

As if Alex needed it. In the ten years he had been the head of maintenance at Gator Glades, every single person he had met who specialized in crocodiles, from herpetologist, to zoo-keeper, to big-game hunter – they had all told him the same thing: do not *ever* turn your back on a crocodile.

Just lately, the park-department had brought in a new Australian guy to help supervise the hybrid clean-up project – a fellow named Clive Whitaker – who had worked with big crocs all his life, and he had told Alex that Florida's alligators were "like little puppy dogs compared to a saltwater crocodile."

It wasn't like listening to shark-experts, or people who worked with big cats or any other large predator, who always seemed to downplay the potential danger – people who specialized in crocodiles had no illusions.

Those that did, Clive explained, were dead.

Alex often watched the crocs at feeding time, and had seen them gather whenever anyone came to the edge, just as they were gathered now, their frog-like eyes following his every move.

There were a lot more than there used to be.

And they were *all* hybrids.

A lot of reptile parks purposely hybridized crocs, specifically *because* of hybrid vigor – they got bigger, faster, and were a more impressive tourist attraction. But Gator Glades had always eschewed such practices as unethical.

Now they had an entire man-made lake dedicated to nothing but hybrids fished-out of the Everglades. The site was still under construction, with a large crane towering above, looming like a giant skeletal Brontosaurus over some prehistoric swamp. The perimeter was lined with stegosaur-like steam-shovels as they continually widened the existing pond to accommodate its ever-increasing population – a consequence of unforeseen circumstance.

Because, while a lot of the problems with invasive species in the Everglades might have come about by accidental release, the situation with hybrid crocs had come from deliberate breeding.

All it took was one backwoods crazy.

William 'Ol' Bill' O'Neil was a local legend – but definitely not in a good way.

Living in a cabin at the furthest reaches of the habitable Everglades, he was listed as a 'gator farmer', although it turned out gators weren't all he was breeding out there alone on the swamp. He was deep into the black market trade, growing exotics of all kinds, but crocodiles in particular.

It turned out he had also been releasing them in the wild for years.

One of his charges – a saltwater/Nile croc hybrid he called 'Caesar', had grown over twenty-feet – and once released out onto the open water, he had started eating people.

Caesar, along with another, not-much-smaller hybrid named 'Nemo', had been the targets of a month-long manhunt.

Both big crocs were currently stuffed and mounted in the Gator Glades' administration building/exhibit-hall's front lobby.

Alex often stopped at the mounted display – labeled 'MAN-EATERS'.

'King Caesar' was posed in a lunging strike with his massive jaws open, and Alex always found himself looking into the giant creature's dead eyes.

It always gave him a chill.

A lot of large crocs in captivity tended to be man-eaters – at least the ones captured in the wild. That was why they were caught in the first place.

As both Jen and Clive had repeated constantly, *every* croc was a man-eater, given the opportunity.

Alex kept that clearly in mind as he made his way up the dock to the pump house.

Out on the water, the crocs followed him along – the dock was where they were fed, and they had learned a human on the dock meant food.

The hybrids in the pond weren't nearly as big as Caesar or Nemo, nine or ten-footers mostly, just cresting the edge of sexual maturity, with the largest of them probably under twelve feet long – although that was still a formidable animal that could leap out of the water its full body-length, up to the base of its tail – nearly twice as far as a big alligator could – which was one reason Jen stressed that Alex maintain his attention around the water.

It was also another reason why he needed to get this drainage pump fixed promptly – they were getting into the storm season and they didn't want the water level rising to the point that some of the more ambitious crocs might be able to reach the dock.

Alex opened the door to the pump house and he could smell the burnt motor. He cursed under his breath. That meant replacement parts rather than just a clean-up job, and probably at least two more hours on the job. He hoped they had all the necessary components on-site.

He glanced out at the water, where the crocs gathered below the dock, some of them rearing their heads up out of the water expectantly, eyeing the toolbox he carried at his side, perhaps recognizing it as similar to the buckets of fish and frozen chickens they were fed out of.

As reptiles go, crocs were smart, and their memories were uncanny. They were like a very simple program that recalled where every morsel of food they'd ever eaten had come from.

That was one of the problems that had developed in Australia – and to a lesser case, with gators in Florida – people feeding them off of boats. In Australia, an entire industry had emerged – 'croc tours' – where big saltwater crocodiles were deliberately lured right up to boats, and fed for the benefit of the tourists.

Clive was critical of such businesses. "A dangerous practice," he said. "Crocs learn quickly that boats and people mean food. And they don't much care whether it's a fish on a pole, or your arm.

"Of course, some of them." he said, "just have that look in their eye. Like they want to have *you*."

He had whistled a few bars from an old children's song, and chimed, "He's imagining how well you'd fit within his skin."

Alex shivered, looking over his shoulder at the goggly eyes gathered around the dock.

Setting his toolbox down, he turned his attention back to the job at hand. He flicked the power switch and got nothing but a groan from within the drainage pump. Power was going in, but the motors were dead.

The pond was simply too full, and the filter was getting overworked. According to Jen, the plan was to expand the pond significantly, as well as lining the edge with concrete walls, cutting down on the debris. As it stood, it wasn't much more than a dug-out mud hole with fencing.

Currently, the project was on brief hiatus while supplies were being shipped in. Depending on how long it took, they might have to add some kind of auxiliary back-up to take the pressure off the main pump, just to keep the water-levels down, especially if they couldn't get it done before the rainy season started.

Alex shut the power off, stepping back out of the little pump shed.

As he did so, he slipped on the dock.

His heart jumped as he caught his balance, grabbing hold of the open door.

Alex laughed a little to himself, glancing out at the crowd of beady reptilian eyes that stared up from the water. No need for stupid moves like *that*. He could already hear Jen chastising him.

He stepped back as he closed the door to the shed.

As he did so, he tripped over the toolbox that he had set down behind him on the dock.

He fell backwards over the edge.

Even with the elevated water-level, it was still a six-foot drop – Alex had time to feel the dip in his stomach and curse himself for a fool before he hit the water with a splash.

He thrashed briefly to the surface, but the dock was hopelessly out of reach.

Even before the first of the vice-like jaws latched hold of him, he knew what was about to happen.

The last thing he saw was Jen, as she came running out of her office, racing towards the dock, shouting the alarm, already far and away too late.

Then Alex tasted muddy water as he was dragged under.

He had time for a single scream.

CHAPTER 2

Jen arrived at work early the next morning, pulling into the Gator Glades' parking lot before the second round of news cameras could get there.

She had been up late last night, watching herself on the news – cuts from interviews with police and reporters, and then standing outside the ambulance as it drove off with what was left of Alex' body.

As she parked her car, she saw she wasn't the only one in early. Her administrative assistant Jerry's car was in its spot, and as she let herself into the main office, she heard the TV on in the break room.

Jerry turned his head as she came in.

"Hey," he said, his face sober and sympathetic. "You're on."

Jen recognized the woman reporter on-screen – a trite little piece of fluff who had actually already visited Gator Glades the week before as part of a promotional walk-through, and who had descended on yesterday's events like a vulture on a still-bleeding carcass.

"This is Ashley Wells," she was saying, her face dramatically grim. "Tragedy struck yesterday, as maintenance worker Alex Kintner slipped and fell into the crocodile pond at the Gator Glades reptile park."

Jerry, an avid conservationist to the point of a compulsive disorder, winced.

"They're really milking it," he said. "That's the third time they've run the same clip of her saying that." He shook his head. "People shot, car wrecks every day. Disease, fires, but one person gets killed by a crocodile..."

"The already scandal-ridden theme park," Ashley Wells continued, "has now suffered the death of an employee."

Jerry cringed.

"Scandal-ridden," he repeated painfully.

The images on-screen cut to yesterday – flashing lights from the ambulance as they loaded the covered stretcher aboard.

Jen shut her eyes. The shape under the sheet indicated the bare minimum leftovers of a corpse they had been able to retrieve from the pond.

The entire incident was caught on video, recorded by security cameras – sound and everything. The footage was currently being reviewed by the authorities.

But Jen needed no review – she had seen it all quite clearly, first-hand. In fact, she doubted there would ever be a moment when the vision was more than an eye-blink away.

She had been watching from the window in her office the moment Alex tripped and fell into the pond. Jerry had been thirty-seconds behind her, and they both came running down to the dock.

From there, they stood and watched Alex torn to pieces – watched helplessly as the crocs fought and tore at their prize, tossing pieces of meat up in the air, and then snapping the loose chunks down their cavernous gullets. The paramedics had fished what was left out from under the dock with a boat hook.

Alex had worked at the park for a long time. When he hit the water, he would have known what was coming.

Perhaps that was the part that bothered Jen the most.

The media chaos had started shortly after the emergency vehicles arrived and lasted for most of the rest of the day.

When it was all over, Jen had gone home alone to her just recently empty house.

There had been a text-message on her phone: "Are you okay?"

From Daniel – Ranger Reid, head park ranger – and until two weeks ago, her live-in beau.

She had almost called him back. It took an act of will not to. Instead, she sent him a brief message: "I'm fine."

They had only spoken in official capacity and very brief texts since Daniel had (temporarily?) moved out.

He had been respecting her space – much to the delight of Jerry, Jen thought archly, glancing at her assistant, who had rather inappropriately asked her to dinner the very day after Daniel left – just as a friend, of course, in case she 'needed to talk'.

Jerry puzzled over Jen's relationship with Daniel, whose perspectives as a park ranger were not exactly the ecological mainstream.

Truth be told, that *was* a sticking point – Daniel looked at too much conservationist activism as focused on the concern of animals over people – a stain of thought that Jen would admit *had* leaked itself into the community – on the more radical end, even manifesting as an outright hostility to the human race itself. There were those who would call you a 'speciest' for favoring people over any other animal.

But for Jen, that didn't mean 'do not support conservation', or that a species shouldn't be protected just because they could be dangerous. At the very least, one should not overstate the danger.

She also believed that humans *were*, in fact, highly destructive to the ecology – sometimes foolishly, sometimes deliberately.

As she crested into her mid-forties, Jen found herself at a crossroads. She and Daniel had known each other as friends for ten years before they ever became a couple, and so they had started their relationship at a very advanced stage. There were already certain expectations in place.

And while their recent blow-up had been almost their only major fight, it *had* been significant – highlighting underlying issues that had to be dealt with. For the moment, they were currently sitting in stasis, but long-term decisions would need to be made soon.

That was why she hadn't called him last night – it would have been for the wrong reasons.

In the meantime, she had work to do and responsibilities to meet, pending an investigation into the death of an employee.

Gator Glades already had its share of problems long before yesterday's incident. Jen had only moved up into management of the park by default. Ashley Wells wasn't exactly wrong when she called the park 'scandal-ridden'.

As it turned out, the former owner/proprietor, a man named Robert Wesley, a local businessman and town councilman, had been involved in the international black market trafficking and breeding of exotic species – operations that had not come to light until after he had abruptly disappeared.

Most suspected his illicit business connections, many of whom operated out of Central America. Criminal enterprises in the region were known for their gaudy and brutal methods of handling recalcitrant business interests.

Jen, herself, had an alternate theory – one that involved a particularly trashy little swamp nymph by the name of Abigail O'Neil.

She and Jen – as well as Daniel – had history.

'O'Neil' – as in, the long-estranged daughter of the very same "Ol' Bill' O'Neil who accounted for most of the hybrids interned on the Gator Glades premises today.

Legend had it that Ol' Bill also accounted for quite a few missing persons out on the Glades. And as legend had it, most of those had been fed to his crocodiles.

There was also the abiding fact that authorities believed Ol' Bill's breeding operations were connected to

Wesley's own illicit dealings, and that Ol' Bill's own untimely demise was likewise related.

Jen suspected Abigail had surmised as much as well.

She also suspected the acorn didn't fall far from the tree.

Jen had voiced this suspicion once to Daniel, who had talked around it to the best of his ability, with the not-too-subtle suggestion that it was a road she didn't want to look down – as close to an affirmation as Jen needed.

In any case, Robert Wesley was gone, and Gator Glades was now under new ownership. Jen thought the park would end up being annexed by the city. Instead, a private-investment corporation had picked them up, an outfit called Natural Wonders Investments.

Jen had looked them up on-line. They were involved in a lot of wildlife enterprises specializing in conservation. Moreover, they seemed to focus specifically on dangerous species – sharks, big cats, polar bears, and now crocodiles. They supported anti-hunting legislation, financed a number of non-profits, and sponsored a lot of media and messaging around the same subjects.

Since they had picked-up ownership of Gator Glades, a lot of new money had been being pumped into the park. The expansion of the hybrid pond was just one example. The general overall infrastructure was getting a make-over, everything from the parking lot to the auditorium stands. Even the old, gaudy giant crocodile jaws that once adorned the walkway into the park were removed – for reasons of 'bad-taste' according to the corporate memo. Gator Glades these days was state-of-the-art.

Jen supposed she should be happy, but it made her a little uncomfortable – she didn't trust not knowing exactly who she was working for, or what their ultimate motives might be. Especially after learning the truth about Wesley.

Last week's TV show promotion was a good example of the sort of thing that gave her doubts. Jen had received a communication from Natural Wonders' corporate office 'encouraging' an interview with that Ashley Wells fluff – and Jen had been even less impressed when she met the woman – a pretty little west-coaster, who hosted a weekly pseudo-documentary TV show called 'Monster Hunter' that produced pieces on dangerous and/or scary animals, ranging from sharks to killer whales – Jen seemed to remember hearing that in the first episode, she'd been bit by a Humboldt squid. She was currently acting as guest-anchor for a local affiliate while she produced a segment on Florida's 'Monster Croc Invasion'.

Jerry had done a histrionic double-take when he heard the working title.

Before the interview, Jen did a brief search on Ashley Wells, and pulled up her promo-page – a long line of bikini shots that seemed to be her primary qualifications as an on-camera reporter. Perhaps that was the qualification someone high-up at Natural Wonders saw in her too.

At any rate, her interest in Gator Glades was on-camera interviews with experts and some footage of live crocs.

Acquiescing to her unseen corporate masters, Jen consented to be interviewed and had given the on-camera tour, introducing Miss Wells to Gator Glades' cast of reptilian characters.

And it *was* an impressive cast.

Most impressive, of course, was King Caesar himself – stuffed and mounted right out in the front lobby, with his world-record-breaking stats posted on a plaque – twenty-two feet, twenty-four hundred pounds. And right beside him, also stuffed, was Nemo – nineteen feet, nineteen-hundred and seventy-seven pounds.

Both man-eaters, raised by Ol' Bill O'Neil, himself, and then released into the glades. No one was sure what their true victim-count over the years might have been, but after the point the authorities became aware of the two big crocs, they had tallied at least four between them.

The bullet holes in their heads had been carefully doctored – which was another unsolved mystery – both animals had been briefly put on exhibit, live, at Gator Glades, and someone had broken into the park and shot them both.

They had one of the incidents on video – the security cameras showed a slight, hooded figure making their way onto the property.

The police had no suspects, and as both crocs had killed people, including a little girl, there was not exactly a human cry to find the culprit.

Jen, however, again had her suspicions – and that was another path Daniel suggested she shouldn't go down.

Yet, Jen couldn't help but be reminded every single day at work, as she walked past the two mounted crocs and their taxidermically-hidden bullet holes.

Of course, Gator Glades featured many imposing *live* denizens as well – Jen introduced Ashley Wells to a whole menagerie of venomous snakes, an assortment of the most dangerous in the world – giant king cobras, gaboon and lance-head vipers, deadly black mambas and taipans.

Giant constrictors were also well-represented, by anacondas, Burmese and African rock pythons.

And of course, there was Buffy, their resident twenty-five foot, three-hundred pound reticulated python.

Like crocodiles, pythons were often hybridized at reptile parks, and then over-fed to make them grow. And while they had no hybrid-serpents at Gator Glades, ever since Natural Wonders had taken over, there had been a 'recommended' uptick in feeding schedule of the big constrictors, to 'benefit the animal' according to corporate memo – another thing Jen had not commented on when Ashley Wells had brought up the subject.

Jen was of the opinion that their catalog of big reptiles was already impressive enough. Florida was a near-perfect habitat for herps – time and indeterminate growth took care of the rest. Over-feeding wasn't necessary – just maintaining the simple health of the animal was enough.

They had several gators over twelve feet – *very* large for the species – as well as a similar number of crocs over fourteen feet – Nileys, mugger crocs, as well as American crocodiles.

The current king of the castle, however was a big saltie named Brutus, who had his own pen, and a live feeding show, where Jen would dangle him chickens off a stick, urging him to leap dramatically out of the water half his length. Brutus was just under seventeen-feet long – although Gator Glades' promotional page advertised him as twenty feet.

Jen found that both irritating and silly – twenty-feet seemed to be the go-to fictional length assigned to any big croc – big sharks too, from what she had seen. But the truth was, seventeen-feet made Brutus one of the largest pure-blood saltwater crocodiles in captivity – probably *the* largest in the United States, assuming all the other advertised twenty-footers at other reptile parks were similarly exaggerated.

Currently, the largest saltwater croc in captivity was an individual named Cassius – as in 'Cassius Clay' – an eighteen-footer living in Australia. A park in Thailand boasted a bigger, nineteen-foot, two-thousand pound croc named Yai, but he was a saltwater/Siamese hybrid.

In point of fact, while there were many very large skulls on record, there had been only one known twenty-foot non-hybrid saltwater crocodile ever actually measured, and that was Lolong in the Philippines – another man-eater captured and put on display for a year before dying of pneumonia developed after the stress from capture.

Brutus' enclosure featured one of Gator Glades' newest acquisitions – another product of Natural Wonders' funding – a 'croc cage'. Just like cage-diving with sharks, guests could pay to go underwater with a saltwater crocodile right there in the park. Similar cages had been developed in Australian reptilian theme-parks.

Jen had offered Ashley Wells the opportunity to film from the cage, but the young reporter had rubbed her arms self-consciously over her light, but long-sleeved blouse and declined.

"I prefer not to get in the water with dangerous predators," she said.

Jen had shrugged. She certainly wouldn't begrudge her *that* policy.

But Ashley had other things on her perky, sensationalist little mind as she segued into Gator Glades' newest feature – the hybrid-croc pond – and of course, its relation to the infamous Ol' Bill O'Neil and his connections with Robert Wesley.

"Wasn't William O'Neil an employee at one time?" she had asked.

Jen had sighed. In fact, Ol' Bill had been caretaker when Jen herself had started on at the park, almost twenty years before.

"He was let go," Jen replied, "after being discovered feeding the crocs after hours."

Jen said nothing else, but it had actually been Jen herself who had caught him, and to this day, it remained one of the creepiest moments of her life – the way he had turned and stared at her, speculatively, his eyes as unblinking and emotionless as the crocs in the pond.

Daniel had suggested Jen was lucky she had been behind a gated door.

Jen herself had no doubt that this was so.

"Considering the connections," Ashley Wells continued, "between Mr. O'Neil's breeding operations and Robert Wesley, what responsibility do you think Gator Glades has to bear for the situation here in Florida?"

Jen knew she was on camera, and avoided scowling with effort.

The 'situation' was one that had been building for a long time, but had metastasized only recently. Although the Everglades had long been under assault by invasive species, it seemed that Ol' Bill's hybrid crocs had just suddenly become a major problem.

It took crocs a while to grow, but a full generation of hybrids was reaching maturity. And with crocs, those few years between adolescence and adulthood made a big difference – not just in size, but in diet. It was the transition between eating fish and predating upon larger, land-based mammals at the water's edge.

In short, the crocs were now big enough to look at humans as food – and people were being attacked.

That was bad in a region used to alligators, which were predominately fish-eaters and mud-rooters, with approximately half the leaping range of a crocodile – people simply weren't cautious enough around the water. Even American crocodiles, indigenous to Florida, were primarily fish-eaters.

Not so with salties, or Nileys – let alone a hybrid. Not once they got big enough.

And as Jerry pointed out, the attacks were also bad from a publicity standpoint – bad for Gator Glades, of course, but also bad for conservation.

Besides the actual human danger, there was the compounding factor of fear that would have the already-frightened public clamoring for the heads of every reptile on the swamp – most of them not even knowing the difference between an alligator and a crocodile, let alone the significance of a hybrid.

"Gator Glades is no longer under the ownership of Robert Wesley," Jen replied, looking into the camera. "The criminal acts of Mr. Wesley were his own. As far as Gator Glades goes, we are doing our best to clear out as many invasive species as we possibly can."

Jen had ended the interview abruptly at that point, declining to take Ashley Wells over to the hybrid pond.

Corporate may have wanted the publicity, but Jen was certain Miss Wells wasn't going to give them the kind of exposure they were after.

But after yesterday, there wasn't going to be any avoiding it.

And as if on cue, Ashley Wells came on the screen again, repeating the same opening line. Jerry glanced over his shoulder.

"She called, by the way," he said. "There was a message on the office voicemail this morning. She wants an interview."

Jen scowled. Of course she did.

The park was closed to the public today, at Jen's discretion. The staff needed a day off. Truthfully, she did too. It was only her own overdeveloped sense of responsibility that had brought her in this morning. She wanted to be available for the authorities, and she still hadn't heard back from the corporate office.

That did not, however, mean she had to grant any more interviews.

Jen had known Alex Kintner a long time. She wasn't ready to see his death exploited for publicity whether it was damaging to Gator Glades or not.

Certainly not for an episode of Monster Hunter.

Even as she thought it, her phone beeped in her pocket. Jen sighed.

Getting ready to be irritated, she glanced down at the screen, but it was Daniel's number flashing.

Jen paused, wondering if the message was business or personal. Daniel was still the head park ranger, and official liaison between the park and the local government.

But when she tapped the screen, she saw it wasn't a text, but a link to the latest weather bulletin – a big storm was moving in.

A park like Gator Glades needed to keep abreast of the weather – animals needed to be locked down, not only for their own protection, but to prevent the possibility of escape.   Usually, Daniel and his staff would aid in the process.

It would be the first time they would have seen each other in two weeks.

And perhaps a good pretense to start the conversation that they needed to have.

Jen was about to return a text when her phone beeped once again.

This time when the name popped up on the screen, Jen frowned.

The incoming message was from Abigail O'Neil.

CHAPTER 3

Deep out on the water, in the remotest part of the Everglades, Daniel had a fourteen-foot crocodile by the tail, when he heard his phone beep in his pocket, followed by Jen's ring tone.

He and Clive were in the process of wrestling the big croc into a holding pen. Daniel glanced down at his hip – Jen was probably calling back about the storm and wanted help on the park's lockdown. But then the ring tone was followed by an 'urgent' notification signal.

After what happened yesterday, Daniel found himself wondering what might qualify as 'urgent'.

At the moment, however, he had his hands full of about half-a-ton of hybrid-croc – he would have to call her back.

Ironically, the immediate area was one of the few places out this far that got reception – the cabin of Ol' Bill O'Neil.

The local government had legally purchased the property, and the park-department had converted it into a field office, on the strength that it was one of the only standing structures this far out on the water.

It also turned out Ol' Bill was a lot more tech-savvy than they might have given him credit for – the cabin was completely internet-fitted, with a satellite on the roof – all perpetually powered by solar panels.

For this and other reasons of convenience, the park department had acquired the property, via an undisclosed agreement with William O'Neil's one surviving heir, his daughter Abigail, who, Daniel understood, had been well-compensated.

The cabin itself occupied the last-habitable piece of solid turf before the glades broke out into open water, separated only by grass marsh and trees, stretching almost all the way to the southwestern coast of Florida.

Even more importantly, Ol' Bill had a fenced gator pen, which they put to use as a staging area for captured crocs before they could be sent to the park.

Currently, the pond was full.

Daniel and Clive had been checking traps all morning. They'd taken the park department chopper – with Clive currently being the only pilot on staff – flying out over the water before landing the bird on pontoons in the lagoon outside Ol' Bill's cabin. They would then go by boat out to retrieve any crocs that had been caught. Once a number of animals had been caught, they would bring a larger boat out to transport them out to Gator Glades.

The fourteen-footer Daniel and Clive were currently wrestling was the largest animal they'd pulled out all week. Once a croc got over twelve-feet was when they really started putting on bulk – the difference between a ten and twelve-footer was demonstrative – the animal started becoming *really* powerful.

Daniel guessed this animal weighed close to a thousand pounds – he and Clive both strained as they hauled the beast out of their boat up onto the bank above the pen, all four of its legs trussed, its eyes hooded, and the snaggle-toothed jaws roped shut.

In his pocket, Daniel's phone beeped again.

"That your lady calling?" Clive asked, and Daniel smiled a little – Clive always referred to Jen as 'your lady', as if to make sure there was no confusion.

Daniel nodded.

"She'll have to wait," he said.

Together, they dragged and tugged the fourteen-footer's full weight up the slope, even as it lay deceptively docile, as crocs will do once you cover their eyes.

The urgent alarm on his message continued to beep.

Daniel glanced at his pocket.

As if sensing the moment of inattention, the big croc gave a lurch, lashing its tail, trying to start a death roll, and nearly wrenching Daniel's grip loose.

"Mind on your work, my friend," Clive cautioned as they held the fourteen-footer still until it subsided. "A sneaky bastard like this is just waiting for your mind to wander."

Clive smiled grimly.

"A guy I worked with in Darwin is missing two fingers and half the hand that went with them, because his attention strayed with a *six*-footer." He nodded to the monstrous animal between them. "*This* guy will take all the rest of you."

Daniel knew it well-enough. Especially how they could fool you. Their lethargy was deceptive – a half-ton animal might lay dead-motionless for hours, yet could still suddenly explode like an activated spring.

And if you were in range when that happened?

"It's like electricity," Clive said. "When the switch is off, there's no problem. When the switch is on, it's already too late."

They had caught this fourteen-foot croc in a trap, although Clive told stories of pulling even larger beasts into boats with just a harpoon and a rope.

"That's how you have to do it down on the rivers," Clive said. "You can't shoot them anymore."

Boat-trapping for crocodiles was usually done with a three-pronged harpoon, with its barbs attached to ropes. You sank the barbs into the thick, bony plates behind the croc's neck, and then you dragged it in. Once you got close enough, you slipped a rope around its jaws, taped 'em shut, and then just hauled the critter on board.

Clive snapped his fingers.

"Easy as cake," he said. "Biggest one we ever pulled out by hand was over sixteen-feet. It took three of us to get him on the boat."

Daniel knew by personal experience the power such big crocs wielded – he had engaged Caesar himself in a one-on-one tug-of-war from the end of a harpoon line before that big croc was finally captured.

It was a battle he would not have engaged in by choice – the animal's power was almost not to believed.

Even this fourteen-footer was far-and-away the equal of both him and Clive together. The trick was to treat them like the reptiles they were – let them move and tire out, and then manipulate them during the periods of lethargy between each energetic burst – because if it caught you in the middle of one...

Well, it was like electricity...

The two of them finally managed to drag the big croc to the top of the bank above the pond, maintaining a good fifteen feet from the water on the opposite slope, before cutting the ropes away from its feet, pulling the strap away from its jaws and the covering from its eyes.

Both men hurriedly backed off as the croc thrashed and made for the water, sliding in with a splash.

The surrounding water answered as dozens of crocs, which had been lying absolutely invisible beneath the surface, made way for the big newcomer.

"That's a good catch," Clive said, pulling out his own phone. "I'll call Huey and Dewey."

The speaker on Clive's phone answered immediately on the first ring.

"This is Officer Jacobs."

"Hey, Darryl," Clive said. "We just pulled out a fourteen-footer. The pen out here's getting a little crowded. Once the weather blows over, can you and Palmer get out here with a boat and start hauling them back to Gator Glades?"

"Might be a couple days, sir," Ranger Jacobs replied. "If the storm causes flooding, we might be getting a lot of calls."

"Understood. But we don't want this pond getting much fuller either."

"Okay, sir," Jacobs agreed.

Clive hung up, nodding to Daniel.

"What did Jen call about?"

Daniel pulled out his phone, but found the battery running low. He indicated the cabin.

"Let me run inside and charge up," he said.

Clive nodded. "Go on ahead. I'll lock up out here." He turned to the pond, staring out at all the goggly eyes blinking back, just at the surface.

"Okay, you bloody buggers," he said, "let's pack it in for the day."

Daniel smiled as he turned back towards the cabin – Clive Whitaker was a good man to have at your back out here.

He was a croc-wrangler from way back, raised in the Australian outback, a PhD in herpetology, who had variously been employed in his younger days as a chopper-pilot, wildlife guide, and game hunter, he had spent years pushing for the conservation of crocodiles, both in Australia and Africa.

Clive was philosophical about that now.

"I still believe it was a good cause at the beginning," he had told Daniel. "Croc numbers were so low after hunters nearly shot 'em out in the last century. But what we didn't understand was how fast they would bounce back again. And they never lifted the protections once they did.

"Now," he continued, "there are crocodiles appearing where they haven't been seen for a hundred years, and people aren't expecting to find them there."

He shrugged. "And for a guy like me, it's time to take responsibility for them being there. Because people are getting killed."

Daniel nodded. He himself had supported protections for Florida's alligators up until his second year in college when a friend's arm was bitten off by a big gator while swimming across a canal. The young man would have died, but Daniel was at that time a pre-med, with designs on being a paramedic, and he managed to stem the blood loss enough to allow time for the Life-Flight chopper to arrive.

"Too many experts," Clive said regretfully, "assume the role of 'activist'. By definition, that kills their objectivity. And it inevitably follows that the science which defines their expertise is compromised."

Clive shook his head.

"Back in northern Australia, saltwater crocodiles have become a real problem. The protected population is booming, just like your alligators in Florida, but salties are a *lot* more dangerous.

"When I was working game management, out of Darwin, they brought in a croc-expert from one of the local reptile-parks. Apparently, because *my* saying so didn't count. And I'll give the guy credit – he properly diagnosed the problem. Because the rivers were overpopulated, it was forcing the smaller, mid-sized crocs out into the surrounding estuaries and streams – many of them in places that are now suburbia. And you've got popular swimming holes that have now become crocodile territory.

"But," Clive said, "this was where his path and mine deviated. He made a point to discourage the '*easy* solution of just going and shooting them all'."

Clive shook his head.

"In his *expert* capacity, he recommended that hunting was not the solution. Based on the logic that, unless you could kill every single crocodile, the streams would still not be safe.

"But," Clive said, "the nugget of truth there covered up the fact that, at base point, he just *liked* crocodiles, and he didn't want anyone shooting them. I could just see him calling up mental images of the unrestrained mass slaughter in the fifties."

Clive eyed Daniel meaningfully.

"That's the corrosive influence of bias," he said. "The whole problem is based on overpopulation in the rivers, but he suggests that because the obvious solution of culling wouldn't be a *one-hundred* percent solution, it shouldn't be utilized at all. A no-brainer, but it's coming from an 'expert'."

Clive shook his head.

"For crying out loud, it's not about 'shooting them *all*'. It's about reducing the pressure on the river that's forcing the stragglers into the streams.

"I *told* them that," he said. "In fact, I suggested to the game management board that the entire problem could be ninety percent solved with a hunting season and a lot of bullets."

"And what happened when you told them that?" Daniel asked.

Clive shrugged.

"Well, here I am. What do you think happened? They fired me."

Daniel nodded. That was *too* telling.

The administrative-level, game-management community in Florida was dominated by just exactly that same sort of mindset.

In Daniel's view, that was a romanticized rather than realistic view of nature. You had to accept the dangers, but that didn't mean you were obligated to put up with them. The whole point of human-society was based on protecting its own – particularly the population that was specifically targeted in areas of high-croc predation – women and children, doing chores at the water's edge.

Clive had no patience for it.

"Pretending otherwise is simply denying a dangerous reality," he said. "It's like Jen's assistant-guy. That wormie little twerp back at the park. What's his name?

Jerry." Clive scowled. "They really seem to believe they can make a problem go away by eliminating bad press. Like calling shark attacks 'negative encounters'. It's insane."

But he sighed.

"On the other hand," Clive allowed, "having said that, the first point is still correct. Those crocs *are* out there now, and in enough numbers that you practically *can't* shoot them all out, even if the political will existed. There's always going to be a straggler. You have to implement other means as well. Public education always helps, but you can't count on that. There are options like electric shock charges along croc-streams."

But Clive frowned, shaking his head.

"You see, that's the thing that so many people just don't seem to get. The places where crocodiles kill the most people are third-world rural, and it's just because of how people have to live.

"Westerners," he said, "and by that, I mean modern-living folks, because there's plenty of them all over. They all assume a human privilege where it simply doesn't exist, and they impose their first-world sensibilities on people who have very little choice about it.

"Australia," Clive said, "has more deadly snakes, more dangerous sharks, larger and more aggressive crocodiles than Africa, but the numbers are a couple dozen versus thousands of fatalities a year. The difference is that your wife isn't walking down to the river to do the wash every day.

"Of course," he corrected, "there are still tribes of Aborigines that live off the rivers. Ask them how they like the explosion in the croc population. They may allow that crocodiles are part of the land, but they don't have any illusions about them either."

Daniel nodded. Most cultures that lived close to crocs had learned to be philosophical about them.

"But Africa along the Nile is much worse. A village I was staying at had a boy grabbed," Clive said. "I was there on behalf of the local game control, attempting to set up a series of nonlethal deterrents. We all heard the mother screaming. One moment, her little son was standing right next to her, and then he was gone.

"Another woman," he said, "in that same village was missing her arm. She got grabbed in exactly the same spot. And you don't have to go far to find these stories either. One person tells you about a croc attack, you've got ten others right there behind."

Clive shrugged.

"That's how things are in Africa. Life is cheap there. Cheaper than anywhere in the world. I've seen fishermen out with hand-drawn nets, right in among herds of hippos, standing in boats that are no more than hollowed-out logs, maybe three feet across.

"They're out there every day. And the crocs come for their fish. And when they get big enough, they come for the people. They've learned they're going to be there."

Daniel could only imagine that kind of life day-to-day.

Florida, however, had its own unique situation, as modern sensibilities seemed to have actually begun to undermine basic survival instinct – people were so preemptively secure in human dominance, that it never seemed to occur to them what it might mean to slip back down the food chain.

The only people that seemed concerned about pushing *back* against the predatory side of nature were those that had lost arms or legs – or children.

And these days, not even all of those – Daniel had talked to more than one maimed survivor, extolling the virtue of living with the environment.

Except the Everglades' environment was no longer natural – and it was a lot scarier than it used to be.

Predictably, the area just around Ol' Bill's cabin had proved to be especially rife with invasive species – all of them pointedly deadly. Before Clive had been brought in, one of Daniel's rangers, a young guy named Laurence, was bitten by a black mamba, which he'd mistaken for a garter snake. Fortunately, Venom One, located in Florida, was stocked with stores of anti-venom for just such exotic species, and they were able to save his life.

Ranger Darrell Palmer had come on-board after Officer Laurence had resigned his post.

It was the crocs, however, that were the more pervasive, ever-present threat.

What they discovered was a whole generation of both Nileys and salties, as well as hybrids of each, all reaching sexual maturity, almost all at once. None of them were yet full-grown, but many of them were over ten and twelve feet long.

Right at the point they became truly dangerous.

"There's no such thing as a 'rogue' crocodile," Clive said. "They're ALL man-eaters."

And locally, they were showing it.

In recent weeks, there had been a deluge of incidents – people being attacked anywhere from in their boats to their backyards – and instead of gators, residents were now finding crocodiles waiting in their swimming pools – one man was even grabbed while lying on the beach when a big saltie just walked right up out of the surf.

The man in the pool escaped with injuries. The man on the beach was never found. So far, that was the only presumed fatality this season, but there had been nine reported attack instances in the last three weeks – most of them, fortunately, still involving smaller crocs, but they were all growing fast.

And human beings were not the only species feeling the sudden predatory pressure – livestock was taking a hit in the rural areas – a fifteen-hundred pound prize bull got taken from a local rancher right out of his herd's watering hole.

Not even other predators were immune – a video was released of what appeared to be a pure-blood saltie with a large bull shark in its jaws. Another showed a big croc with its teeth clamped onto a fellow invader – a fourteen-foot python.

But what really got people up in arms was when it was discovered the sea-going crocs were also taking sea turtles.

Many property owners on the beach set up infrared cameras to catch the activity of endangered turtles on their shores – one of them caught the image of a big croc tearing a turtle apart, cracking the shell with its powerful jaws, ripping out the innards.

That particular video created more viral outrage than the attacks on humans – a sentiment that Daniel found rather troubling.

But at least there was growing public awareness of just what the Everglades faced, and how dangerous the situation already was – not to mention the kind of obstacles, both natural and red-tape, that stood in the way of people like himself, tasked with fixing it.

For example, they had no way to tell which crocodile eggs were invasive species or hybrids just by looking at them. The protected American crocodile made a nest just like any other croc.

Caesar and Nemo had been out there for a long time, and would have been breeding for years with the indigenous American crocs – an endangered species.

Although, Daniel thought archly, American crocodiles flourished all throughout Central and South America. They were only 'endangered' in Florida – and they were currently making a boom recovery there as well.

Nevertheless, because of their status, he couldn't just cull up the eggs when he found the nests. They had to test each individual batch. So Daniel would mark the nest's location and bring one egg back for testing, before he could clean out the nest.

It was this sort of thing that had lent fuel to his blowout with Jen.

Daniel was having a bit of an existential crisis – not a midlife issue, exactly – it was more like he just didn't seem to fit in the world anymore. And while every generation has its own priorities, for Daniel, it was as if his very concept of common sense was no longer mainstream.

It seemed to be a widening chasm – and it put Jen too often, and too far on the other side.

Their perspective on each other had changed, and with it, the dynamics of their relationship had been altered as well.

In regards to the dangerous situation that had been created within the entirety of the Everglades, Jen was determined not to lose her idealism.

For his part, Daniel would not have suggested she do so – only to question where she focused it.

When Caesar had still been stalking the area, the big croc had taken an eleven-year-old girl paddling in a canoe. Daniel had pulled her remains from the swamp – nothing but a head and arm. In areas of croc-predation, it was often just the head of the victim that was found.

In the case of this little girl, it was what her mother had to identify.

Two weeks ago, there had been another close call. This time, a twelve-year old girl had been attacked at a local swimming hole.

The girl's father had told Daniel the first off-note was when their dog refused to go in the water, and stood at the bank barking.

Then his daughter had been grabbed and pulled under. Miraculously, her father and brother had waded in and managed to fight the ten-foot croc away.

Daniel had been on the scene when the ambulance had taken the little girl to the hospital – he had seen her injuries, the fear in her eyes, and in her father's.

And he couldn't help but remember the glazed, dead-look in that other little girl's eyes after he had found her twisted in among the weeds, floating, bobbing on the water-surface.

When things had heated up between him and Jen later than night, it was already on his mind – which was probably why he threw it in her face.

That day's attack had been on the news when Daniel arrived home. Jen had been watching the commentary, and perhaps this had slanted things south, because she was really replying to the TV when he walked in, and she remarked how this didn't change the need to protect endangered species.

Poor timing, poorly chosen words – and for one of the few times in his life, Daniel found himself genuinely angry with her.

The conversation started badly, and got quickly worse, both of them shouting.

"That little girl today is lucky to be alive," Daniel had barked hotly. "She's in the hospital right now." He looked Jen in the eye. "Maybe *you* can go down there and tell her and her father how vital apex predators are to the environment."

He leaned close.

"The *last* little girl was torn apart and eaten," he said coldly. "Maybe you should call *her* mother too. Ask her what it was like identifying those last few little pieces of her eleven-year-old daughter."

It was a deliberate low-blow – intended to hurt.

It touched a button too.

Without reply, Jen balled-up her knuckles and slugged him dead in the face. She could hit damned hard too, and she landed another one before Daniel thought to defend himself.

The second shot actually staggered him and Jen was winding-up for a third, when, without even thinking about it, he reached out and hit her back.

It was just a backhanded slap, but Daniel was broad across the shoulder and the blow knocked her off her feet.

There was a moment of dead silence, Jen looking up in shock from the floor, Daniel looking down in horror at what he'd done.

He reached to help her up but she kicked back and screamed at him.

"Get out!"

Without a word, he had left. Since then, he had been staying in a motel, and spent most of the last two weeks hating himself. He had never hit a woman before in his life. He never would have believed the first would have been her.

It certainly wasn't the way he'd expected the conversation to go that night.

He had gotten up that morning planning to come home and give her the ring he had in his pocket.

Two weeks later, he still kept the ring in his jacket. They hadn't spoken in person since.

And now today, an *urgent* message.

After the events at the park yesterday, that had him a little bit worried.

It was probably just about the incoming storm, he assured himself.

Daniel trundled across the adjoining foot bridge from the croc holding-pond to the cabin.

He paused, regarding the building itself.

Ol' Bill's Cabin – spoken in the formal, proper-noun status. It had been one of the last privately-owned homes this deep into the protected swamp – something the local government was doing its best to phase out completely.

Initially, the plan had been to simply tear the building down, but practicality won the day, largely due to the situation Ol' Bill himself had left behind.

As the extent of his breeding operations were only now coming to be known, it stood to reason that the cabin's facilities still remained useful – besides the holding pond, there were several sheds outfitted with snake-cages and terrariums, all powered and heated by solar – more evidence of that incongruent swamp-rat and his tech-savvy.

In a way, the old man was a bit like a croc himself – clever where you don't expect.

Ol' Bill – a local legend.

But not in a good way.

Just another monster in a swamp that was full of malevolent beasts.

Stories about Ol' Bill went back for decades – right up to the time they found pieces of him inside one of his own pets, pumped out from the stomach of Nemo, after that roving croc was finally captured.

Daniel himself had been to the infamous 'Hanging Tree', where Ol' Bill supposedly dangled his victims over the water – at a glance, a harmless tire-rope-swing hanging out over a large limb, but in function, a sacrificial altar.

Or so rumor had it.

Now they worked out of his cabin.

Daniel was not too proud to admit it gave him the creeps.

He always felt just a little tingle when he let himself in, as if he were trespassing into a local haunted house – the kind that every neighborhood had – the old abandoned wreck at the end of the street, with a past that was... unsavory.

They still used Ol' Bill's computer station, which looked so bizarrely space-age in the rustic setting. Daniel plugged in his phone, and sat down, waiting for it to charge. On the desk, the monitor sat idle, emitting a solid neutral screen, lighting the dim cabin in eldritch blue light.

It brought back a few personal memories of the place as well.

Mostly of the woman who had grown up in this little shack out here in the middle of prehistoric nowhere.

Daniel remembered vividly how that same screen had glowed, on a dark, stormy night more than four years ago, now – that same electric blue – mirrored by the flashing bolts of lightning in the sky above. It was the one night he had ever spent in the haunted house.

His one night with Abigail.

It happened back when he and Jen were still indulging their repressive platonic gentle-fiction, but the fact of that night remained more than a little retroactive sore-spot between them.

It was a night Daniel never spoke of, but also never forgot.

Being with Abigail, in the middle of the primeval swamp, with nature's raging fury blowing all around them...

... it was *primal*.

That was something he could *never* say to Jen, because, what they had was great – but it was very *human*.

And speaking of that...

Daniel felt for the ring box in his pocket.

The two of them would have to talk soon, he resolved. He glanced at his phone, now at eighty-percent charge. He shifted back in his chair, patiently.

As he did so, the chair leg caught on that single loose floorboard, the way it always did.

Today, for whatever reason, just his constant movement across the floor, or perhaps the changing season causing the wood to swell, it seemed to jut up more than it had. Pushing the chair aside, Daniel examined the floorboards beneath the desk.

It appeared one of the planks had shifted out of sequence with the row next to it.

But as he looked closer, however, Daniel realized it was an entire patch of floor that seemed to have shifted.

Now he pushed the desk aside.

"Well, I'll be..." he breathed.

Underneath was a hatchway cut right into the floor, leading below the house.

It had been cleverly hidden – and the effort was telling.

Daniel reached for the latch, hesitating briefly as he remembered whose cabin this had been.

What might Ol' Bill be storing in a hidden compartment under his own house, miles out in the middle-nowhere of the glades?

Daniel had visions of rotting bodies – sick killer's-trophies of some kind – or maybe a nest of cobras. Whatever it was, he was certain it was something he wouldn't want to see.

He took a moment to question his own wisdom before investigating a dark hole under a murderer's floorboards, wishing there was some 'authority' he could call.

Unfortunately, as head park ranger, this was all under his jurisdiction – *he* was the authority.

Cautiously, reluctantly, he pulled open the hatch door. The unused hinges creaked like failing car brakes.

The first thing that hit him was the smell – heavy and turgid – the smell of swamp and decay.

Then a light switched on, illuminating a tunnel below the house, and a stairway leading down.

CHAPTER 4

Jen frowned at her phone as Abigail's name blinked back at her.

After a moment, she tapped the message.

"We need to talk," it said.

Why? A dozen possible reasons flitted through Jen's head, not one of them good, and some potentially a *lot* worse than others.

Her next text to Daniel would suddenly be carrying a little hidden weight. In the last few seconds, the world had just gotten a lot more complicated.

Daniel had sent her the link to the storm report, and Jen had been about to message back, asking for the parks service's help with the lockdown, securing the park's fences and cages. The construction equipment would need to be secured as well.

Usually, Daniel was quick to volunteer his rangers, and probably already had Officers Jacobs and Palmer on call.

Gator Glades normally carried a maximum of fifty employees at the height of the tourist season, from vending and food service, to medical attendees, maintenance and custodial staff, a few administrators, and of course, croc wranglers and reptile specialists.

Currently, they were shorthanded across the board. The summer help was going back to school, which accounted for a significant portion of the daily staff – Gator Glades tended to attract a lot of the herp-majors, who did it for the experience around live animals. Remaining staff took the opportunity of the seasonal lull to go on their own vacations.

Today, minus a couple of security and custodial/maintenance staff, Jerry and Jen were the only two people on-site. With the park closed, most of the guest-service employees would be staying home.

Still, Jen was almost grateful for the incoming weather – it gave her a legitimate excuse not to answer phone calls, and the storm itself might actually draw the press' attention away from Gator Glades.

But it meant a busy day – the weather-link indicated the main blow would be sometime tomorrow night, or the following morning. That gave them time, but they would have to get to work securing the outdoor exhibits, which were primarily the big crocs and gators. Most of the snakes and lizards were already housed indoors, and would simply need to be locked up.

That went for most of the croc enclosures as well. The problem area was the hybrid pond. The crocs themselves would be safe enough from the storm – they would simply stay underwater. But the pond itself was still in the construction stage, and while the surrounding fence was sufficient to keep the crocs in, it was not a permanent structure intended to withstand severe weather.

The last weather bulletin was still calling it a tropical storm, and not a hurricane, but it was nevertheless a lot of water and heavy winds coming in.

Normally, that would not be a problem, as far as any of the animals in the park escaping – there were three layers of fences to get past. There was the fencing around the enclosures themselves, a second around the customer viewing area, and then the main fence around the perimeter of the park itself. Gator Glades had ridden out hurricanes before, with little damage.

The first line of fencing at the hybrid pond, however, was sketchy.

Also problematic was the drainage pump. Alex had been supposed to fix it. The hybrid pond's water-levels were already high, and they had a lot of rain on the way.

Jen was not worried about any crocs making it out the front gate, but if the pond flooded, they could quite easily find a few on the top deck in the morning. Hopefully, Clive or someone could hook up a back-up pump.

But they had to hurry. Jen prepared to set it all in motion.

This was her job as administrator, and these were all real, practical problems – perfect for keeping her mind occupied and off of what had happened yesterday.

And on a purely selfish note, perhaps it might also provide sufficient cover to finally initiate the heart-to-heart with Daniel she had been building up to for days. She hadn't called last night due to the circumstances, but now she thought she was ready.

It was time to tell Daniel what their fight was really all about.

He thought she was mad because he'd hit her. Or hit her *back*, to be perfectly fair, but that was really the least of it. Jen herself, actually felt a bit bad about that part – it almost made her laugh – the look of shock on his face, looking at his own hand as if he couldn't believe what he'd just done.

Jen couldn't believe it either. But to be perfectly honest with herself, if he hadn't, she would have been a little bit disappointed.

Over the years, during what Daniel not-quite-jokingly referred to as their *platonic-period*, that had been one thing that held her back – Daniel was never enough of a rogue – always too much the Mr. Rogers 'nice-guy' – or even worse, a brotherly sort.

Jen was educated enough to recognize what that said about her own psychology. Her sister, Sally, had offered up a few suggestions of her own, and Jen had almost slugged *her* over a couple of them.

Sally's basic premise, minus her colorful sisterly vernacular, was that Jen was mostly a 'good girl' herself – but maybe just a little bit of a brat.

Her sister had also pointed out that their fields overlapped because he was trying to save people – Jen was trying to save animals.

"So who has the higher moral ground?" Sally had asked.

Jen's eyes had narrowed at the open-ended insinuation. Sally was living quite affluently on the settlements of two divorces and two kids. And she just *loved* Daniel.

Whatever Sally thought, however, going forward, two other very large factors couldn't be ignored.

As ridiculous as it sounded, the first was because of their conflicting views on endangered species in regards to apex predators. Jen wondered if there had ever been another couple whose major problems were based on the preservation of giant reptiles.

But the truth was, their fundamentally-held beliefs on the subject put them at odds professionally, and by extension, in their daily lives.

It was becoming harder for Jen to simply accept his viewpoint.

The problem was, that if she were to acknowledge any validity there, it would be to recognize that many of the things she herself had long-believed might actually be destructive and wrong, or had *become* that way, regardless of first-intent.

When Daniel had thrown that little girl's death in her face, it had touched a nerve.

A nerve connected to the second, larger issue.

Jen had found out literally that same morning that she was pregnant.

She had been cranky and hormonal for weeks, and then she had woken up throwing-up. She had taken a home-pregnancy test and then gone to see her doctor the following morning.

Jen had intended to tell Daniel when he arrived home that night. Then that second little girl's attack had hit the news – a survivor this time, but the all-day coverage of the incident, combined with the hormonal cocktail already percolating in her bloodstream, left her emotional and upset.

She knew Daniel would be too – he had fished the last little girl out of the glades – the one who hadn't been so lucky.

Daniel had pulled a lot of bodies out of the water, but that one still bothered him. Knowing that, Jen probably should have been more prepared.

But then he had brought up that little girl's mother, identifying her by her head and arm.

That was when she had hit him – the suggestion that she had *any* responsibility for what that grieving mother saw.

It touched a button alright.

Because now she was going to be a mother herself.

Jen wondered how much worse Daniel would feel if he knew he'd struck her while she was pregnant?

She smirked just a little – a small, evil part of herself filed this away, as potential leverage to be used later.

In the meantime, she still hadn't told him.

She had been about to on that very day, two weeks ago. Then she was going to tell him again today – figuratively, and literally, on the eve of the storm. Her hand had literally been reaching for her phone to start it all off with that first text.

And then Abigail.

After four years.

A sexy little mate-eating spider who had briefly drawn Daniel into her web – a one-night fling that had happened back when Jen still had him cordoned off in the friend-zone.

Now Polk Salad Annie was apparently back in town.

But why in *God's* name would Abigail be calling *her*?

The timing couldn't possibly be worse.

And maybe *that* was why.

Just because she was an evil bitch.

Jen paused, indecisive, looking down at her screen.

She brought Daniel's number up first.

But before she touched the screen, Jerry poked his head in her office.

"Jen? There's someone here to see you. They say they're from corporate."

Jen blinked.

Corporate? In the three-plus years Natural Wonders had assumed ownership, Jen had never met anyone from corporate.

Was this over what happened to Alex?

Jerry stepped aside, ushering in a large, square-shouldered man, dressed in a nondescript black business suit. The man sat down, offering a professional smile. Jerry glanced at Jen uncomfortably, before discreetly stepping out and pulling the door shut behind him.

"Miss Summers," the man said, "my name is Anthony Charles Cross. I represent your employers, Natural Wonders Investments, but more specifically its primary share-holder, Mr. Colin Mason."

Jen frowned. The name rang a bell. But not in a good way.

"Is this about yesterday's accident?" she asked. "We're cooperating with the official investigation. The security video has been turned over to the police."

Cross shook his head.

"Actually, this is unrelated to yesterday's unfortunate incident," he said. "What we're really looking for is information about your former employer, Mr. Robert Wesley. You see, we are conducting sort of an internal investigation into his disappearance."

"Well, Mr. Cross," Jen said, "I suggest you talk to the police."

"We have," Cross said. "And we are not satisfied with the results of their investigation." He eyed Jen meaningfully. "We take responsibility for our own, Miss Summers."

"What do you think I could tell you that the police haven't?" Jen asked.

"It's actually not you that we want to talk to," Cross replied. "We were more interested in whether you had any knowledge of the whereabouts of a woman named Abigail O'Neil?"

Cross' eyes were watchful.

"You know her, I believe?"

Jen kept her poker face, deliberately not looking at her phone.

"I know her," she allowed. "But I wouldn't know where to find her. I haven't seen her in four years. We're not exactly friends."

Cross nodded.

"I see," he said. "And what if I should talk to Ranger Daniel Reid? I understand he was acquainted with Miss O'Neil as well. Do you think he might have knowledge of where to find her?

Jen's eyes narrowed, wondering if she was being baited.

"I don't imagine he could help you either," she said. "But there's nothing stopping you from asking."

Jen stared back neutrally. Cross smiled.

"Well, then," he said, as he abruptly stood from his chair, reaching in his pocket for a card, which he laid on Jen's desk. "Here is my number. Please feel free to contact me with any information you think might help."

He glanced back as he turned to the door.

"I might be in touch," he said.

"Thank you, Mr. Cross," Jen replied.

He nodded and left.

Jen turned back to her phone.

It seemed she wasn't the only one with ideas about Ol' Bill's daughter.

She was for-sure going to need a face-to-face with Daniel after this.

But before she brought his number up, her phone rang in her hand – an incoming call, this time.

The name on the screen was Abigail O'Neil.

Jen frowned.

On the second ring, she touched the receive button and said, "Hello? This is Jen Summers."

"Jen Summers," Abigail responded brightly. "It's been a long time."

It was her alright.

"Abigail?" Jen said. "What's this about? A man was just in my office looking for you."

"Yes, I know," Abigail said. "I've been keeping tabs. It looks like you've finally met your new boss. At least, at secondhand. That guy is one of Colin Mason's corporate goons."

"Who exactly is Colin Mason?"

"I hadn't heard of him until a few months ago," Abigail replied. "Turns out, he's not a good man to know. And definitely not a good man to have aware of *you*."

"What's this about?" Jen asked again.

"We need to talk," Abigail said. "You and me and Daniel. I need you to meet me out in the Grotto tomorrow."

Jen frowned. She was asking to meet Daniel now.

"Where the hell is the *Grotto*?"

"Sorry," Abigail said. "I forgot who I was talking to. You probably wouldn't know it. It's a little red-light district just outside the Wetlands. One of the last spots where you've still got pavement."

A red-light district in the swamp-ghetto, Jen thought. Perfect.

"There's a bar called the *Rooster* on the strip. Meet me tomorrow at two."

"Why? What's going on?"

"Trust me," Abigail said. "It's important."

"Why can't you just tell me right now?"

"Maybe," Abigail said, "because there are things I don't want said over the phone."

And with that, the line abruptly disconnected.

Jen sat a moment, looking down at the phone.

There was a tap at her office door, and Jerry poked his head in again.

"That big guy left," he said. "*He* was from corporate?"

Jen held up his card, which read simply: 'Anthony Charles Cross, Natural Wonders Investments'.

"That's what he said."

Jerry eyed her. "Want to talk about it?"

Jen smiled politely.

"I'm fine," she said. "Why don't you get started on the lockdown. I'll see if we can get some help."

Jerry nodded, closing the door behind him.

Jen picked up her phone and touched Daniel's number.

CHAPTER 5

Colin Mason had spent the day on his yacht, sitting at anchor near a small island in the Keys, exactly twenty miles off the coast of Florida. It was Mason's own private island, not subject to the United States law enforcement jurisdiction. Not that Mason ever went to shore – his boat was his sanctuary.

A young girl lay stretched-out topless on a lawn chair up on the top deck, but Mason had been below in his lounge most of the afternoon, watching videos.

Foreplay, so to speak.

He glanced through the window after his female guest and thought about calling her down.

Not yet, he decided.

The big screen dominating the chamber was playing and replaying footage of crocodiles.

Mason had an affinity for apex predators. He came from a family of them, his own father barely beating the FBI out of Vegas during the last of the organization days, retiring with significant wealth in southern California.

In his youth, Colin was known as a fierce and ambitious successor to his father's businesses – a reputation that only grew after his leg was bitten off by a Great White shark while scuba-diving in the Farallon Islands off the coast of San Francisco.

It is a humbling experience when a man who dominates the human hierarchy suddenly discovers how helpless he is when placed into nature's food-chain.

Sharks became his fascination – and not just sharks, but Great Whites specifically – the APEX shark.

Likewise with crocodiles – the alpha predator within their own reptilian niche – what drew Mason's attention were the giant salties and the killer Niles. The largest, the fiercest, the most dangerous.

Crocs were actually a much greater practical danger to humans worldwide than sharks – the dangerous species of sharks tended towards deeper water, while crocs hunted right along the river's edge, grabbing animals that came to drink – in third-world countries this meant mothers and children doing chores along the river.

Sharks, and Great Whites, in particular, were also rather finicky eaters, preferring nice fat seals, and would avoid – or spit out – targets that didn't meet their calorie requirements.

Crocodiles, on the other hand, were utterly opportunistic predators, completely amoral, ready to eat anything they could catch. If it saw food, a croc would try and get it.

Always. Every time.

Mason ran through a series of videos showing crocs leaping out of the water after a wide variety of prey – sometimes antelope, sometimes buffalo and bison. One big Niley managed to drown a lioness.

There were even several scenes of crocs attacking elephants – usually due to mistaking the pachyderm's dangling trunk as a much smaller animal dipping into the water. Such encounters usually didn't end well for the crocodile, with individuals sometimes being found high up in tree branches, but one big croc caught a near-grown adolescent male in the soft marsh, and managed to trip it up, nearly pulling it in.

The elephant regained its footing and pulled away, but it had been close – Mason would be surprised if there weren't days when the elephant *hadn't* regained its footing.

There were also videos of crocs *versus* sharks – a conflict that seemed to go both ways, the deciding factor almost always being the universal qualifier of 'which one was bigger'?

One segment showed a severed Nile croc's head washed up on a beach off South Africa – likely a shark attack, most probably a Great White.

But then Mason switched to a video of a large saltwater crocodile with a bull shark in its mouth. He had actually seen many similar incidents out of Australia, but this particular scene had been shot right there in Florida.

The reporter narrating the clip was Ashley Wells – Mason had met her during her low-budget-network days back in California.

Mason smiled. He *liked* Ashley Wells – he'd had her out to his yacht once, briefly – as a guest, of course.

He'd not had the opportunity to entertain her *properly*.

That was something else he would need to take care of on this trip.

He switched the screen again – another video of a croc chasing prey across the Nile River in Africa – except this time it wasn't a wildebeest.

This was the sort of video Mason relied on his underground contacts to obtain – there was actually quite a large market for the material, so there was a lot of it out there, but because of its nature, you had to be cautious where you shopped.

Some might call it snuff.

On screen, it was a man swimming, filmed by someone on shore, who had zoomed in on one of those log fishermen who'd been tipped into the river by a big croc.

Mason smiled at the thought – fishing out of hollowed-out logs, yet someone in the village still had a video-recording device – fairly good quality, too, blown up on Mason's big flat screen.

The person filming the video shouted out urgently in an unintelligible language as the swimming man was grabbed and pulled under, followed by a thrashing tail.

Mason shrugged – that one was kind of nondescript.

There was another, somewhere else along the hundred miles of the Nile – a woman doing laundry grabbed by the arm and pulled in. That one was better – the camera caught an almost comical moment of shock as her arm was seized and she was yanked like a cartoon from the bank.

Mason replayed that one several times.

Then there was his current favorite, from right there in Florida – big Caesar himself had been caught on a public dock security camera, grabbing a fisherman out of his boat.

Mason always watched this snippet of video repeatedly – the big croc was clearly visible as it raised its head clear of the water, poising, targeting the unsuspecting fellow, who leaned with his back to the railing, nearly ten-feet above.

Caesar had leaped, carrying more than half his twenty-two-foot body clear of the water, and snatched the man right over the side.

Beside him, the man's startled companion could be clearly heard, "What the FUCK?"

This had been on Mason's highlight reels for almost four years – he had released it online himself, once he'd acquired the raw copy.

But now he received an alert that he had just been electronically sent his latest acquisition – the footage he'd been waiting on all day.

A private video – his own exclusive preview.

Eagerly, Mason hit download, and in a moment, the security video from Gator Glades appeared on screen.

The resolution was quite good – as it should be, with the upgrades in the park financed by his own fortune.

On-screen, Alex Kintner made his way up the dock, all unsuspecting the gruesome death that was yet only minutes away.

Mason sat and watched, rapt, from the initial screams, to the part where Alex was pulled under, his arms flailing, and then to where you started seeing pieces of him pulled apart, as each croc fought for their share.

The entire raw video was over two hours – Mason fast-forwarded to where the paramedics pulled out the slight, tattered remains.

When it was over, Mason smiled.

"That was pretty good," he said.

He hit replay.

As he did so, he glanced out at the young woman sunning herself on his deck.

For whatever reason, his... urges... were a lot harder to keep in check these days. He had always heard that your passions faded as you grew older.

That didn't seem true in his case.

The girl outside was new and had no idea who he was – it was more necessary to remain anonymous these days – partly for his legal disagreements with US authorities, but also because it was simply more difficult to get 'hired-help' operating under his own name.

There had always been notoriety associated with Colin Mason, but now there was a certain... *taste* that went with it.

An unfortunate incident in California was the catalyst.

A boat carrying a shipment of narcotics – one of Mason's more lucrative operations – had gone down, and was recovered by the Feds. The evidence there was incriminating enough to allow his arrest – and by extension, the search of his yacht.

The evidence there had been... *more* incriminating.

Confirmation of long-suspected proclivities and tastes. Mason wasn't just an appreciator of morbid-media – he was a producer.

Mason liked to film it.

Most of his own highlight reels tended to feature sharks – big Great Whites, which were easy to find near his Southern California base, and were particularly handy right there in the Farallons, where he had lost his own leg.

He had *years* of footage. When the Feds seized his boat, he had lost his entire collection. That had been almost worse than getting arrested – a lifetime's work – although he *had* recovered some of it leaked online.

There were a lot of people, Mason mused, with similar tastes.

Just not all of them had a fortune to spend on it.

Mason was one of those lucky enough to be able to combine his work with his interests. Love what you do, as they said.

His presence in Florida was a perfect example.

Mason had come into town to settle a debt, and by the sheerest of coincidence, he found an alert message on an email contact that had not been activated in years.

People of similar tastes tended to find each other.

Mason's interests had naturally lent themselves to dangerous species of all kinds, and Florida was a mecca for the black market trade. It was hardly his primary money-maker, so much as a hobby that paid for itself, and was lucrative enough to keep the smaller grifters happy – like, for example, a local selectman/businessman who fancied himself a player.

Robert Wesley was a tool – he facilitated traffic.

Mason's real contact was William 'Ol' Bill' O'Neil.

A collaborator of sorts.

Mason was the reason Ol' Bill was protected for so long.

He was also the reason he eventually got put down.

Ol' Bill's own tastes had gotten out of control.

The state of Florida was only just now learning how much.

He had, however, been dead for over four years.

That was not the least reason Mason was surprised to find their private dual-account had been activated, with an email indicating an incoming live-feed.

The two of them had been sharing imagery and video for years, via a simple little homemade APP that automatically forwarded recently-recorded footage every time their joint account was accessed.

Right now, there was new video being sent.

Someone was on Ol' Bill's account.

Mason wondered if it was the Feds, somehow discovering the old virtual trail, and hacking in. Not that it mattered overmuch to him personally – he was already legally barred from entering the country, and they already had a preponderance of evidence.

But it *was* a point of interest.

Then there was the incoming video itself.

One of Ol' Bill's latest projects before he died had been transferring old 'home movies' into digital.

When Mason opened up the first of the incoming files, the image of a young girl came on the screen, no more than four years old – all wild red hair and bright, blinking green eyes.

Ol' Bill's daughter, Abigail.

A sentimental sort, Mason thought – Ol' Bill had documented her life.

Mason had seen some of these videos before – to this day, he had never met Abigail, but he had watched her grow.

He sat through the first video anyway.

When it was done, he hit replay.

The next video was Abigail again – older, this time – a teenager.

Another *incoming* alert beeped, as the email continued to download old files.

Whoever was accessing the account had stumbled onto something new.

When Mason tapped the file, this footage was much more recent.

Mason had provided Ol' Bill all the most modern tech – an advantage in both professional and personal operations – and one of the upgrades was motion-activated security cameras, posted all around the property

– tiny devices hidden in corners, providing a full view of the entire surrounding area.

Over the last four years, these cameras had all continued to operate.

And as Mason was discovering, there *had* been motion on the property in the last four years.

Some of it was pretty good.

And once again, the most dramatic footage featured Abigail herself.

She was grown now – a striking woman, even by Mason's standards.

Mason sat through each file, one at a time.

A couple of these, he played back.

He glanced up at the girl still waiting stretched-out on his deck, all-unknowing of the anonymous rich-guy she had agreed to meet, as she currently enjoyed an extremely luxurious day in the sun, on the ocean.

Mason shut his eyes – his urges were becoming more impulse-activated.

He reminded himself that was what brought Ol' Bill down.

Mason spent another moment admiring the young woman's slender, toned frame, her tanned skin, lying there, utterly at ease.

And having no idea...

Later, Mason thought, turning back to his screen.

Patiently, he searched through four years of video-records – hours of footage.

He watched it all to the end – some of the latest footage was a bit dry – mostly scenes of rangers working on the property, unknowing their motions had activated the cameras, which recorded away as they went about their chores.

The interesting stuff was mostly at the beginning.

But it was *very* interesting.

He played them all back a few more times.

Then he tapped his phone and called the number for Anthony Charles Cross.

Cross answered with absolute formality immediately on the first ring.

"Yes, sir, Cross here."

"Anthony," Mason said, pausing the video, "I have just been sent a gift from the angels."

He smiled.

"I think we may have a bit of leverage on our evasive little minx."

CHAPTER 6

Daniel sat in the dripping, mud-caked hole, lit by electric blue light from the computer screen.

Behind him, fenced-off securely, the underground cave opened out into the water.

Back when Caesar had been captured, it had been ascertained the big croc's lair was somewhere under the cabin. This hollowed-out mud-chamber was obviously it – set up with sunlamps, no less – Ol' Bill, providing maximum comfort for his pet killer croc.

Daniel had seen similar set-ups in some of the seedier dwellings out on the swamp – the same sort of modern tech imposed in patches, standing out in the primeval setting – often rather novel forms of ingenuity from the swamp-rats that lived out on the water. Houses that seemed barely livable were adorned with satellite hook-ups, along with power-cords and twisted wires, inserted into the structure like intravenous ivy tubes.

The ingenuity of the sub-human animal.

It had been four years since the parks department had acquired this building, and they had not even thought to look for the security cameras that were apparently hidden all over the place.

The feed from a few of them had gone out in the intervening years, but most seemed to be up and running fine.

The log records started piling up right around the time immediately after Ol' Bill's death.

Since then, those cameras had recorded a veritable treasure trove of deep dark secrets.

Or perhaps 'secrets' wasn't the right word – perhaps it was more like cold, hard confirmation of things that Daniel had already known all along.

And Ol' Bill kept it all right down in Caesar's lair – perhaps the safest place possible to store illicit material, an underground cave with a guard dragon on duty.

There were several old cabinets resting against the chamber's mud walls, all sealed and water-proofed. A brief inspection revealed old film reels and VHS tapes, along with several VCR players, attached to DVD burners. Ol' Bill had apparently been in the process of transferring old media into digital format.

When he sat at the little desk, perched on the muddy ledge, tantalizingly close to the water, Daniel found a whole cue of files waiting for a prompt.

Had Ol' Bill sat in here like this? Daniel wondered. Under the muddy ground with a six-meter crocodile lying fenced-off, bare meters away?

At the thought, he glanced down at the murky water. With Caesar gone, Daniel wondered what might have been occupying the mud-chamber in the time since.

At the bank, illuminated in the blue light, were fresh mudslides.

There was at least one big croc using the place – probably several, based on the slide-marks. All right next to their storage facility – the owners of those slide marks had probably been watching Daniel and his men working all along.

The cavern was set up as a luxury-cove – solar power was humming, warming the sunlamps, all motion-activated. Power-cables connected up through the floor of the cabin.

It was a bizarre, self-sustaining system. The computer screen clicked on as if it had been last started yesterday.

The image on-screen was apparently the most recent video Ol' Bill had converted, sitting there all this time, waiting to play.

Daniel clicked the video.

It started with a close-up of Abigail as a little girl.

The grainy footage showed Abigail standing on the docks.

After a moment, Daniel realized what he was about to see – Abigail herself had told him this story.

She would have been four years old at the time, already with a wild head-full of red hair, and bright, blinking green eyes – you could already see the beauty she would become.

She was feeding a crocodile off the dock – no doubt Caesar himself in his younger days.

The video clearly showed Abigail tossing the croc a severed human arm.

And then the rest, piece by piece.

This would have been Johnny – former paramour of Ol' Bill's wife, Abigail's mother – a woman, rumor had it, who had not left Johnny for Bill voluntarily.

She was also a woman who had fallen in with Ol' Bill's pet crocs one night – the night Johnny had come back for her and the two of them tried to run.

Ol' Bill had blamed Johnny,

He explained it all to Abigail on camera.

"That's the guy that took your mother from us," he said, pointing to the dismembered pile on the dock.

Daniel swallowed dryly, remembering how Abigail's body had clinched when she told this part – lying in bed, pressed against him in the dark – a story she had likely not often told before.

It was pillow-talk like Daniel had never heard, and of which he hadn't spoken since.

On-screen, there was a brief close-up of Johnny, chopped-up into parts, before the camera was apparently set on a stand.

Daniel watched as Ol' Bill, a relatively young man at the time, showed his four-year old daughter how to first dangle the scraps for the croc's attention, and then to toss the piece into the open jaws as it reared from the water.

The images stung his eyes like chlorine, but he could not tear away.

When the video finished, Daniel checked the menu list.

There were a *lot* of files.

He clicked on another video – this one taken at the Hanging Tree, with its infamous rope-swing – fitted with a tire at the time, which was now long-since gone.

Daniel had no idea who the person in this scene might have been – what had Abigail said was her father's criteria? Someone who had done him wrong? Maybe someone who had come nosing about?

Or just someone random, who got caught alone out in the Everglades.

Daniel remembered Abigail saying her father wasn't a 'serial killer' – he just acted upon necessity.

Just saying that was remarkable – and telling – it indicated a nearly-total unconscious denial.

What Daniel saw on-screen had nothing to do with necessity – this was a *taste*.

Ironically, he found himself thinking about his argument with Jen, and how her views on humans as a species were always so destructive and dark.

Faced with such evidence as was being burned into his eyes today, he found it a harder position to argue.

"Humans kill for no reason," was one of Jen's axioms.

Daniel's response was that humans are just like any animal, and all animals kill for a reason. Sometimes it's territory, sometimes emotion. Animals killed for food, defense, and for survival.

And they also killed for pleasure – some of them just seemed to like it. After all, most mammalian predators grow up developing hunting skills as a manner of play.

Of course, primitive predators were entirely different – they were simply programmed to kill whenever the instinctual trigger was pulled.

That was why crocs were so deceptive – there was no build-up – no Def-con – just suddenly their switch was pulled.

Their hunting mode had no tell – a big croc might stalk prey for days, or even weeks – the strike might be sudden, but the predatory trigger might have been pulled days before.

Not that it mattered to the prey. The fact that there was nothing personal in it for the predator was irrelevant – in the case of crocs, it actually made the situation worse – a croc can't unlearn two-hundred million years of evolution – it was *always* going to behave like a crocodile.

And in a human-environment, that meant there were places they simply couldn't be tolerated.

As far as Daniel was concerned, people had the right to be safe, and if that meant culling out a few competing alpha predators, then so be it.

"Apex predators," Clive had agreed, "are not ecologically necessary in areas where humans exist – that's *our* job."

But based on what he was seeing today, it was clear those predators didn't have to be reptiles.

He could also see where personal awareness made the predation worse.

The next video was Abigail again – older now, just shy of sixteen.

Another pile on the dock and now two crocs waiting in the water below.

Daniel knew this story too.

This stack of dismembered limbs would have been Virgil – Johnny's brother, whose family feuded with Ol' Bill over rumors of what had happened to Johnny.

One night, Virgil had taken it out on Abigail herself – a pretty young teen – chronologically, it would have been bare weeks before this video was taken.

It was the *last* time, she had told Daniel, lying in bed, her nails clinching painfully on his chest, that she had been *taken*. She swore never again.

Her father wasn't about to put up with it either. Ol' Bill had rounded up Virgil, and chopped him up for croc-bait just the same as his brother.

More pillow-talk that Daniel would not forget.

This video was of more modern quality, as Abigail, her movements now confident and sure, tossed each piece of Virgil off the dock.

Caesar was approaching nineteen feet or better, at the time, and he reared up, nearly taking the pieces out of her hand, pushing aside the smaller Nemo, who was still a mere fourteen-footer.

The next file Daniel opened was the first of the security-camera videos, which was apparently programmed to save recordings when the motion-sensors were activated.

Unlike the earlier videos, these images were operating on modern tech. And by the looks of it, there were cameras all over the place – at least two-dozen viewpoints, all over the property, and even out over the surrounding water.

As he blinked through the footage, he found images of both Jen and himself, back when they had first ventured out to the cabin after its owner's arm had been discovered in the belly of a crocodile.

And then their first meeting with Abigail. Daniel turned the sound up for a moment, reliving the event word for word.

Daniel realized what must be coming next, even before he again saw himself, now framed in the electric light of the storm, carrying Abigail across the threshold of the cabin.

And then their night together – all recorded moment-to-moment.

Oh boy, let Jen find out about *that*.

Daniel shut his eyes, fast-forwarding past the images, lest he remember too much himself.

He would be lying if he didn't sometimes think of her, and their night together.

But when he did, he also remembered lying there in her arms, with the storm raging around them, and how she had confessed her sins in the dark.

He still remembered the cold feeling that had washed over him as he realized what kind of creature he clung to – deadly – amoral – a black widow spider.

She had talked for a long time, regurgitating her life.

Daniel suppressed a chill at the memory as those stories she told played out live on the screen before him.

Although, as Daniel continued rummaging, he discovered there were a few stories Abigail obviously hadn't told.

A more recent clip starred Virgil's youngest brother Pete, who was likewise hand-fed over the docks, into the gator pond out back this time.

There was also the hour or so Abigail spent alone with him in the cabin before dismemberment began.

Harsh interrogation, to put it mildly.

And Ol' Bill had been long gone by then.

Necessity, Daniel thought.

He cut back briefly to one of the images of Abigail as a little girl, a severed limb in her hand – reconciling that image as the ground-note in the psyche of the grown woman that he now knew, he clicked back to the image of her as an adult – those piercing green eyes, dark and hard, and sleeves of tattoos webbed down her arms.

She was five-foot two, maybe a hundred-and-twenty lean pounds, but Abigail was one of a few people Daniel had met who truly frightened him.

When you looked in her eyes, there was just something that wasn't there.

You could be fooled by talking to her, because she was bright, displayed normal human emotions, and spoke with a rational mind. She also understood perfectly well what were and were not acceptable behavior codes.

But she was not *bound* by them, psychologically or philosophically.

In Daniel's experience, a person with no boundaries and no restraint was no different than the feral psyche of a wild animal – they were not quite human. You were dealing with a person who might be capable of anything.

He had now seen with his own eyes how capable she was.

She was definitely worth being afraid of.

The hell of it was, Daniel still found himself feeling a bit sorry for her.

And he was at least honest enough with himself to wonder if it wasn't something else as well.

There was no denying she had aroused something primal in him.

But neither would he deny that this had been before her hours of follow-up pillow-talk.

She had aroused the mating urge of the male spider, who follows the female into her nest, even though copulation will eventually mean its end – to be devoured post-coitally by his mate.

Presuming those same lack of boundaries, Daniel wondered what Abigail might do if she knew all these videos existed – or that he himself had seen them.

She might have already told him many of these stories, but now he actually qualified as a witness.

Daniel wondered if it might also be worth it to be afraid of the knowledge he now possessed.

He nearly screeched aloud when Clive suddenly hollered down into the chamber from the cabin above.

"What the hell?" Clive said, "Are you down there, Daniel?"

Daniel clicked off the video.

"Yeah," he called back up. "Looks like Ol' Bill kept himself a den."

Clive paused.

"What have you got down there?"

Daniel shut the computer off.

There were a lot of remaining files he hadn't seen.

"Just some home-movies," he said, glancing over his shoulder at the murky water beyond the fence, and the slide-marks on the bank, as he started back up the stairs.

Clive saw the look on his face.

"Home-movies?" he asked, doubtfully.

Daniel didn't answer, grabbing up his phone, which was now fully charged.

He had two text messages.

The first was from Jen.

It read, "Your girlfriend is back in town."

Daniel now understood the *urgent* notification, and there was only one *girlfriend* she could possibly mean.

And sure enough, the second text was from Abigail.

"How you doing, Ranger?" it read.

Daniel frowned.

"Something wrong?" Clive asked.

Daniel sighed.

"Many things," he said.

He stuck the phone back in his pocket.

"Come on. Let's lock this place down and get out of here."

CHAPTER 7

It was mid-afternoon by the time Anthony Charles Cross made it to the Grotto. According to Mr. Mason, their latest information suggested this was where to find Abigail.

A red-light district halfway between the city and the Wetlands, it would have made Tijuana look like a family resort.

It was also largely separate from the more sophisticated establishments in the urban areas that might have been more under the direct influence of Colin Mason.

"Keep your pants up out there," Mason had cautioned. "The whores have crabs so big you could drop them in a pot and cook them."

Cross parked his car in front of the largest building on the modest strip – the bar and tavern, with the blinking neon sign, the *Rooster,* above. When he stepped inside, it smelled of smoke and sweat, along with the cloying overkill of perfume.

It was still early in the day for the local trades, so the place was sparsely occupied, although not empty.

Cross waited a moment for his vision to adjust to the dimness. When his eyes cleared, several tables were looking back at him over their shoulders – a couple of lone drinkers, a table full of scantily clad females, likely waiting for their shifts to begin at the neighboring establishments, as well as several tables where some of the lone drinkers had already paired up with the dancers.

Ignoring them, Cross made his way to the bar, where a leather-patched dominatrix was bartending.

Before he even sat down, she set a drink on the bar in front of him.

"I pegged you for scotch on the rocks when you walked in," she said.

Cross smiled professionally. That *had*, in fact, been his order.

"Maybe you could help me," he said. "I'm looking for someone."

She smiled. Her name-badge read 'Tammy'.

"Everyone here is looking for somebody," she said.

"I mean a particular somebody," Cross replied. "Goes by the name of 'Abigail'."

Tammy shook her head, still smiling.

"A lot of people go by a lot of different names out here," she said. "Maybe if you had a picture?"

Cross had two, neither of them very good – both blown up from old video, one at age four, one at fifteen. He brought them up on his phone.

"She would be in her mid-thirties by now."

"What can I say?" Tammy replied, looking down at the two images. "She looks like every girl around here, before they got here. Then they all look like *her*."

Tammy pointed to a woman sitting in the corner, nursing a drink and a cigarette, eyeing Cross speculatively. She offered a feline-barfly of a smile and Cross could swear he heard her purr all the way across the room.

Remember those crabs, he thought.

Tammy handed Cross back his phone.

"I'm sorry I can't be more help," she said. "The truth is people don't much like being asked about around here."

"She's right," a man's voice said from behind him.

Cross turned on his stool to find a tall grizzled figure had risen from his table and now stood behind him.

The man was wearing a Sheriff's badge.

He extended his hand.

"Sheriff Leroy Barnes," he said. "I'm the law in these parts. For what it's worth."

Cross offered his professional smile.

"Anthony Charles Cross," he said as he shook Barnes' hand.

The Sheriff sat down next to him

"Can I help you, Sheriff?" Cross asked.

"Just looking out for the citizenry," Barnes replied. "Tammy here's telling you the truth. People keep a good eye on strangers out here. Stranger than the locals, I mean. Or the regulars." Barnes shrugged. "See, folks tend to come here mostly for one reason. Sometimes the other. Both illegal."

"I'm not here for either of those," Cross said.

"I can see that you're not," Barnes replied. "And that's the problem. Everybody can see it. That's why everyone's looking at you. If you're not one of them, or if you're not a paying customer, you better watch your step. People in the Grotto don't like people looking into their business."

At that moment, Cross' phone beeped a message in his pocket. Mason's alert tone.

"Excuse me a moment, Sheriff," he said, pulling out his phone and tapping the screen.

"Forget the Grotto," the text said, "Get out to the cabin."

Cross sent an acknowledgment back.

The cabin. Ol' Bill's cabin.

Sheriff Barnes was regarding him closely.

"Call from the boss?" he asked mildly.

"It was indeed," Cross replied. "Thank you, Sheriff, but I have to be moving along."

Barnes stood.

"Probably best," he said.

The Sheriff tilted his head, nodded at Tammy the bartender, and the cat-eyed woman still staring at them from across the room.

"Take care, Mr. Cross," Barnes said. He turned for the door, lighting the room in a brief glare of sunlight as he stepped outside, and then back to darkness as the door swung shut behind him.

Cross sat a moment, looking down at his phone.

What was the best way to get to the cabin? He'd already mapped the location, but the real question was whether to try and get there by land or boat. The water levels were already high this season, and according to reports, bad weather was coming in – that could mean flooding.

On the other hand, it was getting late – he still had to make it the rest of the way to the Wetlands before he could even rent a boat. He couldn't get one here – the Grotto specialized in a different industry.

Even as he thought it, a feminine voice spoke up behind him.

"Buy you a drink, stranger?"

Cross turned. It was the cat-woman who had been watching him, now sliding into the bar-seat beside him.

"I already have a drink," Cross replied, holding up the scotch Tammy had poured for him.

"Well, drink it," the woman said. "And maybe I'll buy you another."

Cross smiled and tossed the glass in a swig. The woman smiled back.

She had a pretty face, Cross thought. Heavily made-up, with a gypsy-scarf covering her head like a shawl, highlighting bright intelligent, almost luminescent, green eyes.

Eyes with just a touch of the wilding in them.

Cross felt the first burn of alcohol rush into his bloodstream, and with it, just a touch of lightheadedness.

"I'm sorry, miss," he said, "but I really have to go."

Her smile never faded.

"Yes," she said. "Yes, you do."

Cross paused uncertainly at the rather cryptic remark. She stared back with a steamy gaze that was obviously well-practiced.

She did it well, Cross had to admit – and her eyes were striking.

For a moment, he was tempted, crabs or no crabs.

But he had work to do. He knew Mason wasn't prepared to be patient on this one.

Cross stood from his chair, but the moment that he did, he was struck with a wave of vertigo nearly enough to topple him off his feet.

The woman caught his shoulder.

"Careful there, stranger."

Her smile widened – that cat-like smile. She tipped her head to Tammy the bartender who nodded back affirmative.

Cross staggered, gripping for the bar – the dizziness was growing worse, and now his vision was starting to blur.

He looked back at his empty drink glass and realized belatedly what had happened. He reached for the gun in his pocket.

But the green-eyed woman caught his arm, reaching into his pocket and handing his gun to Tammy.

"Ah-*ha*," she said, waving an admonishing finger.

Cross blinked back at her.

It was too late anyway – the world was dimming fast.

"Who *are* you?" he asked.

She smiled brightly, blinking those cat-green eyes, as she pulled her scarf from her head, tumbling out a mane of cascading red hair.

"You can call me Abigail," she said.

CHAPTER 8

Cross blinked awake the way you do after being knocked-out with anesthetic – there was no sense of time passing, no sense of dreaming.

The first thing he came aware of was that it was now nighttime, and that he was tied-up, with his feet bound and his hands behind his back. When he struggled, he also realized he was sitting in a boat. His hands behind his back were attached by a length of rope to the thick, overhanging branch of a large tree.

There was water on all sides – they were somewhere deep out in the swamp.

Sitting in front of the boat, was the woman from the bar.

Abigail.

Ol' Bill's daughter.

She seemed occupied, whittling away at the bark of the tree trunk. But then she saw he was awake. She folded up her knife and smiled at him.

"Mr. Cross, how are you feeling?"

Cross said nothing. Mason paid his people well in anticipation of just such occasions. And Cross had been on both sides, at one time or another.

Abigail nodded.

"Strong and silent. Believe me, I know the type. And I also know who you work for. So I think it's important that we understand each other."

Abigail produced a flashlight, blinking it quickly in his eyes.

"Here," she said. "I want to show you something."

She shined the light out over the surrounding water.

All along the surface, there seemed to be glowing lights, blinking like Christmas bulbs.

"Crocs," Abigail said. "Their eyes reflect light like lanterns at night."

Cross followed Abigail's light as it traveled all around the boat. There was scarcely a patch of the surrounding lagoon that didn't blink back glowing eyes.

Some of them were pretty big.

"There's probably a few gators out there too," Abigail continued mildly. "If there are, they gotta be pretty big ones or else the crocs would have chased them out. They're pretty territorial."

Abigail turned the light back on Cross. He squinted in the glare.

"You know the difference between gators and crocs, Mr. Cross?" Abigail asked. "It's the difference in their prey. Gators are mostly fish-eaters, or any of the smaller critters you find living on the marshes. Crocs are big game hunters, evolved to take the big herd animals that come to the river's edge to drink. Large mammals. Like humans. And they're aggressive about it.

"What that means," Abigail explained, "is that, given the opportunity, a croc *will* kill you and eat you." She smiled. "Not *can* – *will*. They're actually unique that way. Most big predators are actually fine to be around if they're not hungry and not actively hunting. Not crocs."

Cross stayed silent. Behind his back, he was straining at his bonds. He'd been tied-up before, even broken a pair of handcuffs once. Sizing up Abigail, he guessed he had well over a hundred solid pounds on her. If he could just get one hand loose...

Fortunately, she was talking, giving him time.

"I grew up with crocs," she was saying. "My father raised them."

Abigail leaned forward.

"You know who my father *was*, right, Mr. Cross? And do you know what he used to do, right here at this tree?"

Cross looked up at the overhanging limb.

Suddenly, he realized where they were.

And yes, he *did* know.

Cross was not from the area, and had not grown up with the local superstitions and rumors, but he'd dug up an awful lot on Ol' Bill O'Neil in the last few months – and where the public records ended, he had not come up short on people willing to tell stories.

This was the Hanging Tree.

Where Ol' Bill fed people to his pet crocs.

"Yeah," Abigail said, whimsically, "he sure did love those crocs."

She turned back to Cross, and now she held up his own Iphone.

"What I will be needing from you," she said, "is the code to your phone and then Mr. Mason's number."

Cross just stared at her.

Abigail smiled sweetly.

"I know," she said, "that Mr. Mason wouldn't hire someone who'd be intimidated by little old me. So I won't try. I will instead offer you a bargain."

She reached under her boat seat, pulling out a hatchet. With the smooth practiced move of chopping-up a large, slippery fish, Abigail brought the sharp edge down across the front of his right foot, cutting away the top two inches of his shoe, and all five toes.

Cross grunted in the shock of pain and disbelief.

He stared down at his mutilated foot, and the spurting blood.

Then he was overcome by fury, cursing, fighting wildly at his bonds, wrenching his hands, ready to tear them loose.

This brief rebellion only left him more securely bound than ever, as the ropes on his arms actually seemed to cinch even tighter.

Ignoring Cross, Abigail picked the bloody toes out of the severed piece of shoe and, one-by-one, tossed them out into the water.

There was a rush, as several of the smaller crocs chased after the morsels like ducks after bread crumbs.

The muddy water collected in the bottom of the boat was growing thick and dark with blood.

Abigail pulled the hatchet loose from the boat floor.

Then she brought it down again, this time burying it in the boat-seat two inches from Cross' groin.

"I told you that it's important that we understand each other," she said, "so I'll make it easy. This is my bargain. You give me Mason's number, and I won't cut up the rest of you and feed the pieces to these crocs."

She twisted the hatchet in the wood, pressing the edge up against his crotch.

"Starting with this piece," she said.

Abigail shrugged.

"It's up to you. Really, what's the harm? You know he wants to talk to me anyway."

Cross glanced down at the hatchet. Then he read her the code to his phone.

"That's Mason's number," he said as she brought up his main screen. "Right there on the list of contacts."

Abigail tapped the number, pulling up the last series of messages.

She smiled.

"Mr. Cross, you've been very helpful."

She twisted the hatchet out of the boat-seat.

"Therefore, I will *not* cut you up and feed you to these crocs."

She held up his phone – the camera light blinked on.

And then she cranked the throttle and the boat jerked forward, away from the tree.

Still tied to the branch above, Cross was yanked out of the boat, and now dangled above the water.

His injured foot was bleeding like a sieve.

Abigail stopped the boat a dozen yards away, holding up the camera.

"Smile, Mr. Cross," she said.

There was an explosion of water as the first of the crocs burst up through the surface.

Cross saw the teeth.

In his last moments, he was not stoic. He screamed.

Abigail zoomed in as the croc latched onto Cross' leg.

Cross struggled, hanging awkwardly, as the croc began to spin, twisting his arms behind him as he turned on the dangling rope.

Then the water surface broke again, as more crocs leaped up after the prize.

One of them caught Cross' other leg, and now the two crocs pulled together, both turning into their death-rolls.

Cross howled as his right leg was torn loose below the knee.

Abigail kept the camera on him as she steered her boat up next to the tree trunk.

Cross' screams rose to a pitch as a second croc latched onto his remaining leg and together the two of them ripped most of it away.

Abigail tapped up Mason's number, and sent a message with the incoming video.

It read, "Don't come after me."

Then she hung Cross' phone in the little nook she had carved out of the tree trunk, aiming the camera, and letting the recording continue.

Cross' voice had lost the strength for screams – his breath came in the whimpering gasps of a suffering animal.

He didn't beg, like some people did.

Of course, he was probably in some degree of shock, maybe losing consciousness.

But he found his screams again, a moment later, when more crocs began leaping out of the water for the rest of him. Minus his dangling legs, they had to come up higher to get at the rest of him, grabbing hold and hanging on in tenacious croc-fashion.

His arms wrenched behind his back, his lowest point was now his dangling head.

Abigail could hear the jaw-snap as the teeth of a large croc clamped on his skull.

Several others latched onto his remaining thighs, and even pieces of his jacket.

The rope holding him to the tree-branch finally snapped and Cross dropped into the water.

In moments, the crocs were on him.

Abigail heard a last, gurgling wail as he was dragged under.

Within moments, they began pulling him apart.

Notched securely in the tree trunk, the camera recorded it all.

Abigail turned her boat out of the lagoon.

Mason had tracked her all the way to the Grotto. And according to his last message, he had sent Cross out to the cabin.

There were few places out of the reach of Colin Mason, Abigail was discovering – that meant not even the Grotto or the Wetlands were safe. But it was better there than in the city. At least, out on the swamp, home-field advantage was hers.

She had been living off the grid successfully for four years – which wasn't all that hard when you had money. Abigail's settlement for her father's property, as well as the reward money for her role in the capture of Caesar, had left her quite comfortable.

Mason had not been able to find her.

But he had found Jen. And by extension, Daniel.

That might be a problem, going forward.

CHAPTER 9

Mason had an Easter-egg waiting for him.

He had finally brought the young girl down into his cabin with him, and they'd spent the last couple of hours doing exactly what she thought she was here for in the first place.

At one time, Mason would keep the same girl on for years, often several in every city, just simply for the convenience.

Eventually, of course, they all ended up the same way. And these days, they tended not to last long.

Fortunately, for this new girl – who called herself 'Lily', and may or may not have been underage – Mason found himself distracted.

Few people genuinely interested him.

William O'Neil had been one of them.

His daughter Abigail was another.

Mason had been waiting on word from Cross, before he'd finally retired with Lily to his chambers. He had fallen asleep for a few hours when he woke to a message alert from his phone, beeping where he'd left it on his couch in the lounge.

Hiking his one leg out of the bed, he hopped into his wheelchair – hardly a necessity – he could move about on his single limb as well as most people could with two. But Mason liked to play up the handicap – it was deceptive.

He buzzed the automated chair out into the lounge after his beeping phone. He tapped the screen.

It was a text message, with a video attached.

The text read, "Don't come after me."

Mason plugged his phone into the big screen and played the video.

He sat silently, watching, touching down the volume once Cross' screams began, lest they wake Lily, still sleeping, unsuspecting, in his bed-chamber.

When the video finished, Mason smiled.

"That was pretty good," he said.

He hit replay.

Cross had worked for him a long time. The fact that Abigail had been able to take him out so easily, was notably impressive.

She was clearly her father's daughter.

It was a shame he couldn't let this video go public – he would have loved to hear Ashley Wells' breathless, grim analysis.

Mason was still reviewing the video, when Lily finally roused.

"Hey," she said, rubbing her eyes as she walked into the lounge, looking like a sleepy kid – which, basically, she was.

Mason turned the video off.

"Good morning," Mason returned, smiling, regarding her standing there in her panties and one of his t-shirts.

Some days that... itch... was greater than others.

Today, it was strong.

Mason beckoned for Lily to come sit in his lap – she hopped into his chair with him, hugging his neck, as he motored the two of them up the ramp out on deck.

He rolled them to a stop along the railing, where one of his deckhands, a tall, bearded fellow named Rodney, was tossing fish-guts overboard. He waved his bloody ladle.

Lily gagged at the smell.

"Oh, that's awful."

Mason smiled, waving Rodney back.

"My apologies," he said. "But I wanted to show you something."

And with that, he hopped up out of the chair, with her still in his lap – Lily let out a startled *whoop*, as he effortlessly took her whole weight in one arm, standing the two of them up by the railing.

They had left the security of Mason's island behind, and were now motoring out on open ocean, looking out onto the southernmost coast of Florida.

About an hour ago, he'd had Rodney chum-up a pack of sharks.

Lily's eyes widened as she looked at the circling fins over the side.

"Wow," she whispered, "they're *big*."

She glanced down uncomfortably at Mason's missing leg.

Mason smiled.

Back in California, they would have been Great Whites. These looked like mostly bull sharks.

As sharks go, they weren't the heavy-duty turbo-predator that white sharks were, but they were still big, powerful beasts, and worldwide, bull sharks were arguably the more dangerous species.

While a bull shark couldn't hit with the authority of a big Great White, they were pugnacious and aggressive, prone to take largish prey. And while a white shark might leave a clean, albeit large bite, bull sharks were snaggle-toothed and powerful jawed – they hung on and tore at prey, leaving behind ragged wounds that were difficult to stitch, leaving a higher percentage of victims to bleed to death.

Bull sharks also took these traits into close-quarters with humans. They were famous for living in both fresh and salt-water, as well as being a global species. Much like crocs, their true human damage, along third-world river systems was largely unrecorded.

In point of fact, it was Great White and bull sharks together that created the fiction of JAWS – among the spree of real-life New Jersey shore attacks, only the first, out in the surf, was definitively the work of a white shark – all four others, which occurred inland, in brackish or fresh water, were most likely bull sharks.

Off the coast of Florida, there had also been speculation among some experts that bull shark populations were up due to the over-fishing of competing ocean-going sharks.

The ones circling around the yacht were certainly big, well-fed, and fat.

Mason's hand caressed Lily's shoulders as she looked nervously over the side.

His hand stopped just at her neck, running his fingers through her hair – just for a second, seeming to clench, before sliding down her back again – softly, caressing.

The itch was strong.

Mason smiled.

"I had a wonderful time," he said, turning Lily to face him. "But I've got a busy day. So I think it's time we say goodbye."

His hand gripped her shoulder...

... and turned her towards Rodney, who stood waiting patiently for instruction.

"Rodney," he said, "would you please take her back to shore?"

Mason glanced down at Lily.

Maybe next time, he thought.

He had someone else he wanted to meet with tonight.

Lily, having no clue, nevertheless looked a touch relieved.

Rodney led them to their little outboard dinghy.

"We've got to hurry, sir," he said. "I just got a weather report. There's a big blow coming in tonight. We've got to get to port."

Mason considered.

"On second thought," he said, "Take us around the south point. I'll take Miss Lily back myself. I'm going ashore."

Rodney frowned.

"Are you sure that's a good idea, sir?"

"Once you drop me off, take the boat back to the island. And stay in phone contact."

Mason pulled out his phone, checking the weather-link himself.

This was actually working out perfectly.

He tapped out a number, and the call was answered immediately on the second ring.

"Yes, sir," a man's voice said aloud.

"You know what to do," Mason said, simply. "Get it done."

He paused, glancing over the side at the circling sharks.

"Make sure the cameras are on," he said.

Rodney was helping Lily into the side-boat. He looked up at Mason with dutiful concern.

"Are you sure about this, sir?"

Mason smiled, looking down at Abigail's message.

"Don't come after me," it read.

She might as well have hung a lamb-chop around her neck.

"I want some alone time with this one," Mason said.

CHAPTER 10

Daniel had never been out to the Grotto before, although he'd heard raunchy stories about it since high school. He wasn't happy about going out there today.

Jen wasn't happy he was going either – the fact that it was at Abigail's invitation didn't help.

"That woman is out of her mind," Jen had said emphatically. "The 'Grotto'? She wants us to meet her in some seedy red-light district, halfway out to the Wetlands? I am *not* going out there."

Daniel had not answered.

He'd not returned Abigail's text, earlier, instead messaging Jen that he was coming in to meet her at the park. So far, it was not going at all as he'd hoped.

It was the first time he'd seen Jen in person in two weeks and part of him ached just at the sight of her – he never failed to marvel at the understated elegance in her features – she wore little or no make-up, dressed in practical work-clothes, and as she entered into her mid-forties, she bore a bare feathering of wrinkles around the eyes.

She made no effort to tart herself up, yet she attracted the eye with the pure symmetry of her face and form. He'd known her for nearly fifteen years, but he still found himself entranced

But Jen had not exactly greeted him with hugs today when Daniel had walked into her office – in fact, her blood seemed to be up.

'*Your girlfriend called*,' had been her text.

That wasn't a good start.

Daniel cursed silently. He wanted *so much* to reconcile – and when she had first texted him today, he'd had the sense she was ready to be receptive.

But then, out of the blue – Abigail – you couldn't have picked a sorer spot to poke.

"What did she say when you talked to her?" Daniel asked. "What does she want?"

Jen's eyes narrowed.

"It was about that visit I had from corporate today," she said.

She had told him about the visit from Anthony Charles Cross. She also had learned a few things about Gator Glades' new corporate owner.

"I looked up Colin Mason," she said.

She handed him her phone, showing the headlines.

Daniel frowned, scrolling down.

He'd heard about Colin Mason back when he was arrested.

"*This* is the guy looking for Abigail?"

"Yes," Jen said. "And he seems to think that Abigail had something to do with the disappearance of Robert Wesley."

She glared at Daniel.

"Now *why* would he think *that*?" she said, meaningfully.

Jen scowled.

"Psychopathic bitch," she muttered sullenly.

"Keep in mind," Daniel said, "she saved your life. And mine."

Jen stared darts back at him.

Daniel mentally kicked himself – why would he jump to Abigail's defense like that?

Probably the same reason it got Jen's dander up so much – because she had cast a little spell on him.

Daniel couldn't quite explain it himself.

He absolutely never brought Abigail's name up, much less told Jen about her pillow-talk *confessions* – or any of the other things he believed about her.

Or perhaps 'believed' was too soft a word – more like the things he *knew* – and had now seen irrevocable proof of just today.

He suspected Jen had some idea, anyway.

"You're going, aren't you?" she said. "You're going out there to meet her."

"I can't imagine," Daniel replied, "that she would show up if it wasn't important."

Jen held up the phone, with the images of Colin Mason still on-screen.

"Important like this guy?" Jen said. "This is who she's mixed up with."

"And apparently so are you," Daniel replied. "He's your boss."

Jen fell silent a moment. She was still absorbing all the implications there. She shut her eyes, taking a breath.

"Don't go," she said. "I need your help shutting down the park. We need to get locked down before the weather hits."

"I'll be here in the morning. Clive can help. So can Jacobs and Palmer. I'll be back by late afternoon."

Jen pursed her lips, and then finally she said what Daniel knew she was eventually going to say.

"I remember what happened the last time you went out to her place alone."

Daniel felt his own temper click just a notch.

"I'm not going to *her* place. And I wasn't in a relationship then."

Jen eyed him.

"Are you *now*?"

Daniel paused.

"I guess that's up to you," he said.

She didn't answer.

That exchange between them had been yesterday. And things weren't much better today.

Jen had remained silent and withdrawn when Daniel had shown up early that next morning with Clive, Jacobs and Palmer, and they had gone to work locking down the park.

She'd spent most of the morning avoiding him, either in her office or the opposite side of the grounds. But just before noon, Daniel caught her at her desk, eating lunch. She looked up as he let himself in.

"Well," she said, "*you're* leaving."

"I'll just be gone a few hours. We'll talk when I get back."

Jen was cool.

"Tell your girlfriend I said *hi*."

"Jen..." Daniel started, but was interrupted as Jerry poked his head in behind them.

"Sorry," Jerry said, glancing at Daniel. "Am I interrupting?"

"It's fine," Jen said. "How's the park looking?"

"The indoor enclosures are all secured. We're finishing up the last of the outdoor. Clive has got a back-up pump working on the hybrid pond. We won't have time to get the main pump fixed before the weather comes in. Alex was supposed to..." Jerry shrugged. "Well, you know." He cleared his voice. "It should be okay."

"Okay," Jen said. "Finish up and go home."

Jerry nodded to Jen, his eyes sympathetic as he glanced sideways at Daniel.

Daniel caught the look. For just a moment, he felt the tiniest impulse to just knuckle-pop the little bastard.

Jerry ducked back outside.

Daniel turned back to Jen.

"She asked to see both of us," he said.

Jen nodded.

"But you're the one that's going."

Daniel sighed. This wasn't going to get any better. There was no point in prolonging it.

"I'll be back by early afternoon," he said simply and turned to leave.

Jen had not answered.

That had been an hour ago. Now, he was bumping along on the semi-maintained road leading out to the Grotto.

Daniel wished he could explain to Jen why he had to go. But the unfortunate fact was that there were some things he simply couldn't tell her.

The simple answer was, he was going because he was afraid *not* to.

Although, he supposed Jen suspected that as well. Daniel had never boasted much of a poker face – she could certainly see he was anxious.

He had brought his service pistol with him today.

And as he motored along the ostensibly-paved road, he noticed someone was following him about a quarter-mile back.

His paranoia was showing, he thought – he knew perfectly well that the Grotto got a certain amount of traffic and this was the only road out there. There were bound to be other cars.

It just seemed that *this* car was being a little too subtle.

The truth was, he was even more nervous than he let on, and there was more than one reason why.

Daniel had done a little more research on Colin Mason last night.

It turned out Mason was a higher-level bad-guy than Daniel was comfortable dealing with.

But it stood to reason, with the revelation of Robert Wesley's black-market activities, that someone *like* him would have to be involved.

And a guy of Mason's... *tastes*... would naturally be drawn to the trade of dangerous exotic animals.

It was also perfectly feasible, considering the suit-wearing goons already sniffing around Jen's office, that Mason might take the time to put a tail on Daniel too.

As the saying went, it wasn't paranoia if they were really out to get you.

The vehicle behind him was a pick-up, and hovered a steady quarter-mile back.

Ahead, the trees were starting to break up, letting the overhead sun shine through. So far, it was a gorgeous day – you'd never guess a major tropical storm was looming on the horizon.

The Grotto was only just ahead. He saw the first signs – hand-painted ads for some of the local 'businesses'.

He slowed down as he drew closer.

The Grotto was built as far inland as the swamp would allow – the 'highlands', as far from the river and annual flooding as possible. It connected to the Wetlands further on, via an adjoining road that ran along the waterways into town.

Beyond the Grotto, there wasn't much else – people traveling this way mostly had to be going there.

As he slowed, turning into town, the pick-up rolled up behind him.

Daniel pulled off to the side of the road, glancing nonchalantly at the other driver as the truck rolled past.

It was a woman – obviously one of those 'painted ladies' who worked the establishments in the area. Probably on her way to work. She continued up the road, before pulling over herself into a local lot.

Daniel stepped out of his truck, looking down the modest strip for the address he'd been given – the main local bar.

He began walking up the street, looking down at his phone for the name – Roosters – and had actually almost walked right by the place, under the sign, when a voice spoke up behind him.

"How you doing, Ranger?"

Daniel turned, and Abigail was sitting at a table set out on the sidewalk.

At her side was a young boy, maybe a little over three years old.

Abigail smiled.

"Good to see you, too."

CHAPTER 11

"This," Abigail said, ruffling the young boy's hair, "is Denny. I call him 'Little Ranger'."

Daniel stared down at the boy. Abigail blinked innocently.

"He has your eyes, don't you think?"

Daniel was momentarily stunned to silence, when the clip-clop of heeled shoes trapped up behind him. It was the woman in the pick-up. She glanced briefly at Daniel, before extending her hand and the boy ran to her, clutching her leg.

Abigail smiled sweetly.

"Babysitting," she said. She turned to the other woman, "Thanks, Tammy."

Tammy nodded, glancing again suspiciously at Daniel, who was close enough to a cop to be unwelcome on this street, before she led young Denny back to her pickup.

He has your eyes.

That one had nearly given him a heart-attack.

"Sorry," Abigail said, "I couldn't resist. You should have seen your face."

She grinned.

"Too bad your little girlfriend didn't come along."

"Yeah," Daniel replied, with a visible lack of enthusiasm, "that would have been funny, alright."

Tammy beeped her horn as she drove by, with little Denny waving from the front seat. Abigail waved back.

"Tammy is a friend," she said. "She helped me a lot when I was young."

"Showed you the ropes?" Daniel said.

"And then some," Abigail said. "Me and her and a few of our friends still do favors for each other."

"I don't imagine you have to live like this anymore," Daniel said, indicating the Grotto.

Abigail smiled.

"Once a Sister, always a Sister," she said. "That's *this* tattoo."

She held out her arm, pointing to a black-symbol in-between the painted webs. "I was sixteen when I became a member. I made that initiation by the skin of my teeth."

Daniel was tempted to ask the details but thought better. Abigail would probably tell him. Instead, he sat down across from her at the table.

"Why am I here?" he asked.

"Because," she said, "it might be possible your life is in danger. And maybe your little girlfriend too. I thought you'd want to know."

"Why would our lives be in danger?"

Daniel already had a pretty good picture, but he wanted to hear Abigail tell it.

"Turns out," she said, "my father's connections went a little deeper than Robert Wesley. Have you ever heard of a man named Colin Mason?"

"Only vaguely, until yesterday," Daniel said. "Jen showed me some headlines."

"I hadn't heard of him either," Abigail said. "But apparently my father had. And apparently, he's heard of me.

"Tammy," she said, "gave me a call a few months ago. Told me the word was coming down the pipe that he'd put a hit out on me."

She shrugged.

"I've been digging since then. Turns out stories about Mason aren't hard to find."

"So what's this all about?"

"On the surface, it's about the disappearance of Robert Wesley. It might be about loose ends, or he might think I had something to do with it.

"And," she said, "he might think you'd have a line on tracking me down."

She eyed him meaningfully.

"OR, if he thought I cared, you might be leverage to bring me out."

Daniel regarded her curiously.

"DO you care?" he asked.

"I'm here, aren't I?"

"So, why," Daniel wondered, "would he think you had anything to do with Wesley's disappearance?"

Abigail shrugged.

"Mason's crazy. Crazy people get funny ideas sometimes."

She leaned forward.

"And that's what I want to impress upon you. Mason IS crazy. But crazy like a very old and wily, dangerous, psychotic fox."

Abigail pulled out her phone – an expensive top-of-the-line device, Daniel noted – and she started tapping.

"There are a lot of people who kill people," she said. "For a lot of different reasons. Some for necessity, some for business.

"And some," she said, holding up her phone, "do it just because they *like* it. This is one of the videos seized by the Feds after Mason was busted back in California."

Daniel was grateful for the small image. In content, it was reminiscent of the videos he'd watched in a mud-hole underneath Abigail's family cabin, just yesterday – only these videos featured sharks.

It rather resembled Shark Week 'Air Jaws' breaching videos – a human didn't look much different than a seal when blasted apart from below by a two-ton Great White.

"These have all been leaked onto the darker corners of the Web," Abigail said, blinking through several videos in a row.

There were a lot of them.

At spots, there were screams – the volume on Abigail's phone sounded loud in the lazy early-afternoon street. Daniel looked around to see if anyone was in earshot.

Abigail tapped off her phone.

"Do you take my point?" she asked.

Daniel nodded slowly. He was convinced.

If for nothing else, there was the look in Abigail's own feral eyes.

She sat with her arms wrapped around her shoulders as if cold, her taut, dancer's muscles rippling under the mosaic of tattoos spider-webbed along her arms – her Wiccan spirit animal.

Daniel realized Abigail was afraid of Colin Mason. He wasn't sure if it was fear for herself, or for him, or just in general. But Mason scared her.

And that was no mean feat.

Seeing that fear in Abigail's eyes, Daniel felt a cold touch himself.

"What do you suggest I do?" he asked.

"Hard to say," Abigail replied. "Mason's got eyes everywhere. He can't come on American soil. Not without risking arrest, anyway. But that doesn't mean he can't reach you here.

"Someone," she said, "was out here looking for me yesterday. I only told one person I was in town, and that was your little girlfriend."

"As far as I know, she only told me," Daniel said.

"Mason's got ears," Abigail said. "But now he's shown his dorsal. That means he's about to make some kind of move." She shook her head. "The predator doesn't reveal himself without reason."

"And he likes videos, does he?" Daniel sighed.

The connection was obvious.

"Abigail," he asked, "what was his relationship with your father?"

"A sick, psychotic one."

Daniel nodded.

"I found some old videos," he said. "In your cabin. Videos of you. As a child. And some *not* as a child."

Abigail grew still.

"Okay," she said, sitting to attention.

"Apparently," Daniel said, "your father was fond of videos too. He took a lot of home movies. And sometime in the seventeen years you were gone, he jury-rigged the cabin and the entire surrounding area with motion-activated cameras."

He shrugged.

"I just stumbled onto it yesterday – the security camera server is hidden underneath the house. Dug right to Caesar's old den.

"It was still active," he said. "Which means it's been recording the goings-on at your old cabin all along."

He eyed Abigail meaningfully.

"Anything," he said, "that has happened in or around that cabin since your father died, would likely have been recorded."

Daniel shrugged.

"I thought *you'd* want to know."

Abigail nodded slow agreement, her eyes wide and thoughtful.

"Anyone see it besides you?" she asked. "Does anyone else know the chamber is there?"

Daniel thought of Clive. Just by bringing up what he'd found in the mud-hole at all, he was already taking a chance that Abigail trusted him. There was no reason to put Clive on the craps table too.

"Just me," Daniel said.

Abigail gave him a long slow look – a speculative, scrutinizing eye.

"But," Daniel cautioned, "he had it on his computer. I'm not the one to say he never sent it to anyone. Someone else who likes video."

Abigail nodded.

She sat back in her chair.

A brief silence fell between them. It had been four years since he'd seen her – and she looked *good* – healthy, maybe a touch heavier to go with it – not to mention her clothes – while stylistically indistinguishable from the swamp gypsy he remembered, she now wore real silks, and her bracelets were gold.

'Well-compensated' was how the reports had described her settlement with the state for the deed to her father's cabin. The good-life obviously agreed with her.

"So," she said, regarding him, one eyebrow raised, 'how are things with Daisy May?"

Her green eyes were penetrating and attentive as she spoke.

She had a way about her, Daniel thought, of getting you talking – he actually had the impulse to tell her the truth. If he were a younger man, he might have made that mistake – initiating the conversation, allowing her to be comforting, letting him confide – but these days, he understood the mechanics.

"Couldn't be better," he answered firmly.

Abigail laughed.

"You are, without a doubt, the worst liar I've ever seen." She shook her head. "You really are the good-guy, aren't you?"

She smiled, reaching out for his hand. Daniel felt a spark of static crackle as their skin touched, and she gave his hand an affectionate squeeze.

"It's good to know," she said, "when a man can't lie."

Daniel pulled away slowly. He stood from the table.

"I've got to go," he said.

Abigail gave him her big, dark green eyes.

"Take care of yourself, Ranger."

"You too, Abigail."

But as he turned to leave, she called after him.

"Can I call you if I need you?"

Daniel paused, looking back.

He nodded.

Abigail smiled.

Walking back to his car, he could feel her eyes on him.

His hand still tingled where she'd shocked him. The air was heavy and humid, thick with static, practically buzzing with energy.

There was definitely a storm brewing.

When he reached his car, an old pickup was pulled-up beside it in the road.

There were lights mounted, and the lettering on the side said 'Wetlands County Sheriff'.

Daniel recognized Sheriff Leroy Barnes standing beside his parks vehicle. He was smoking one of his God-awful hand-rolled cigarettes that smelled like burning tar.

Barnes tipped his hat in greeting, then nodded his head back in Abigail's direction.

"She's got her hooks into you, don't she?"

"Sheriff," Daniel said, extending his hand formally. "Isn't this a little outside your territory?"

"Actually," Barnes said, shaking Daniel's offered hand, "this little stretch is within my jurisdiction. It tends to be mostly self-contained. All the oldest, most popular sins, at cut-rate."

Barnes took a deep drag of his cigarette. Daniel could *hear* his lungs blackening.

"Of course," the Sheriff continued, "everyone's got different reasons for coming here. Counting yourself, the last couple days, they've been a bit non-typical."

He blew a plume of smoke at a black caddy parked across the street.

"That's been there since yesterday. Gonna tow it tomorrow. Registered to an Anthony Charles Cross."

Daniel blinked.

Barnes' quick eyes caught it.

"Know the name?"

Daniel knew it alright. That had been Jen's visitor.

But he shook his head.

"Someone," Barnes said, blowing another puff of smoke at the caddy, "came and never left."

He took another long drag.

"The swamp's like that. Even away from the water."

Daniel eyed Barnes.

"What's your interest here, Sheriff?"

"My interest," he said, cocking his thumb over his shoulder, "is the same as yours."

Abigail was still watching from down the street.

"She and I go way back."

Barnes finally pinched off his cigarette, snuffing the flame between two calloused fingers.

"The night she ran away from home, just turned sixteen, I found her out on the road."

Barnes shook his head.

"She lost her mother young, and bein' raised by Ol' Bill, that poor girl was never going to have a chance. But she was running anyway.

"I picked her up," Barnes said, "set her up with a little money, an old, abandoned car, and sent her on her way."

"So, you just let a sixteen-year old girl fend for herself?" Daniel asked.

The Sheriff shrugged.

"At least, it was giving her a chance," Barnes said. "One step better than where she was."

Barnes pitched his snuffed cigarette.

"Probably would have lost my job for it, if it'd been found out. What can I say? She didn't seem right for the social services. It felt like the right thing to do at the time. I didn't know why she was running, and I didn't care. I knew Ol' Bill and that was enough."

Daniel glanced back up the street, to see that Abigail was now gone from the table – perhaps into the bar.

He turned back to Barnes.

"I've got to get going, Sheriff. There's weather coming in."

Barnes nodded.

"Been watching that." He scented the air. "Feels like it might be coming in early. Best be getting home myself."

Barnes nodded as he climbed back into his truck.

"Take care, Ranger," he said.

He pulled away, continuing on through town where the road veered southwest towards the Wetlands.

Daniel looked back at the sky to the east, and it seemed as if the horizon was darkening. Barnes might be right – the storm was brewing early.

Hopefully, he could beat it back to town.

He turned his truck around, heading back the way he had come.

As he passed the *Rooster* bar out of town, he glanced at their empty table, but Abigail had gone.

In his pocket, his phone beeped a weather-bulletin.

The storm was still miles off shore, but it had indeed changed direction.

It was coming at them now.

CHAPTER 12

Abigail had not been to her father's cabin in four years – and then seventeen years before that. It had not occurred to her that Ol' Bill might have security cameras.

She'd known about the hole in the floor, of course. Her father had gone down there often and just sat, watching Caesar as the big reptile slept on the bank below. There had been no computer-server in those days – just a man and his pet crocodile.

Abigail had recurring nightmares about that hole as a kid – mostly about her father going down there and not coming back up.

Ol' Bill never brought his daughter down with him – he told her sternly it wasn't safe.

But Abigail thought it was really more because it was HIS space – his den – his *room*.

Where he kept his best stuff.

And he'd apparently upgraded.

If they were really exchanging videos online, Abigail guessed Colin Mason had something to do with the tech infusion – which meant the possibilities were a lot wider than Ol' Bill's own budget – the entire area out by the cabin might be as on-camera as a five-star gated community.

That was bad enough.

Worse was the possibility that some of that footage had made it out.

No longer private-media, as they say.

Abigail took a breath – she didn't know for sure yet, so there was no sense wasting energy on it until she knew the real situation. And she wouldn't know until she got there.

She bumped her utilitarian four-wheel along the ever-deteriorating roadway through the downtown area of the Wetlands, past the last of the paved road. The only paths that led out to the remaining properties and sites this far out in the glades were gravel, dirt or mud – and at the right time of year, underwater.

It was getting close to that time of year, Abigail thought, as she took the old road to the house – and she could see it was definitely the one less traveled. She guessed the parks guys mostly came and went by water. The land route to the cabin was overgrown with disuse.

There were also spots where the river was already crossing the road.

Abigail stepped on the gas, churning muddy water, as she barreled her four-wheel drive straight through.

As she drew closer to the cabin, she started seeing signs – notices posted by the State of Florida – 'No Trespassing', 'State Property'.

There were also 'Danger' signs, some highlighting 'potentially dangerous invasive wildlife'.

Ahead, the foliage began to part, as she came up to the first major split in the river, and made her way over the rickety bridge onto the mini-island that was the property. Another mile down the road was Ol' Bill's cabin.

The cabin itself looked mostly the same.

There were more signs posted along the outside fence, identifying the property as belonging to the state, informing Abigail she was trespassing and risking fines or incarceration just for being there. There were also 'Danger' signs everywhere – some of these marked with symbolic gator-jaws and the bold-print: 'Dangerous Wildlife'.

For almost every other person in the state, it was a horror house.

For Abigail, it was home.

She looked at the shuttered building, braced for the storm. Out back was the gator-pond. And then you were out on open water, for as long as the Everglades went, until you reached the ocean.

A horror house was perhaps not a bad description, considering the goings-on within and around its walls.

But ironically, for Abigail growing up, it was the one place she had always felt... *safe* wasn't the right word... but it was *her* place, where she could hide away from the rest of the world – the deepest swamp, so far away from the eyes of God and man that no one could ever find her.

Turned out she was on camera all along.

Abigail didn't have many illusions, but bizarrely, the knowledge of that fact brought the sting of tears for the first time in maybe twenty years. She wiped at them savagely.

She knew she was likely being filmed at that very moment. No telling how many cameras might be about – some of them probably small as a thimble, all hidden in the nooks and crannies, out among the surrounding trees, even out on the water.

Most of the footage Abigail was concerned with would have been several years ago – after her father had died.

Hopefully, that meant it was video that had not been forwarded on.

Of course, Daniel had seen it too – he had been evasive as to specifically what he'd sat through, but Abigail had a good idea what was there.

She wondered if he had seen her little interview with Virgil's younger brother Pete – that had gone on right there in the living room.

Daniel already knew things about her – things Abigail was sure he didn't want to know.

Which begged the question, how much did Mason *think* he might know?

Abigail was becoming afraid just considering possibilities when it came to Colin Mason.

It had been about six-months ago when she'd got word on just who exactly was looking for her, and exactly what that meant.

Abigail had learned about Mason on-line, but what scared her was the way that people who knew him spoke.

It was rather like the way people spoke about her own father.

The cabin was dark, the windows shuttered in anticipation of the incoming storm. Behind her, the sky was already growing dim, and she could feel the breeze beginning to pick up.

She was actually surprised to find the front door locked.

This was now parks department property, she reminded herself.

She walked around to the back. If she couldn't get in there, she'd break a window.

As she circled the cabin, her eyes strayed to the gator-pond – a *croc* pond, now, actually – a holding tank for invasive and hybrid crocodiles. She wondered how many of them there were.

Abigail frowned as she peered through the rain.

The gate to the pond was standing open.

Ranger Daniel Reid wasn't the type to leave things sloppy like that. The pond was dug steep on purpose, but with the gate open, any one of those crocs could climb right up the embankment.

And if there was flooding – like might be the case tonight...?

Abigail walked around to the back deck.

The first thing she saw was a boat docked – an outboard dinghy-type – it looked expensive – definitely not parks department.

Then she realized the back door to the cabin was standing open. It looked to have been kicked in.

Electric blue light shined from inside.

Abigail hesitated – she had left her rifle in her truck. She was about to turn and get it when a man's voice stopped her.

"Miss O'Neil, please come in."

Cautiously, Abigail leaned in the back door and looked into the cabin.

Colin Mason was sitting at her father's old desk. He had the computer screen on in front of him.

He looked up as Abigail entered, and he smiled.

"Well," he said, "you *have* grown up nice."

CHAPTER 13

As hurricanes go, it was more of a tropical storm.

It didn't even warrant a name, and was actually not expected to do that much damage.

Unfortunately, it just happened to abruptly change course and charge directly for the coast. The force of wind was relatively minor, but it struck inland with its full strength, and it brought a lot of rain, and with it, a lot of generalized flooding.

More significantly, it also brought up a storm surge – or a meteorological tsunami, depending on which meteorologist was quoted in the days that followed. It was not a notably *big* surge, no more than ten feet deep, and penetrating barely a quarter-mile inland.

But Gator Glades reptile park was right on the coast.

CHAPTER 14

Jen was on her way home when the rain started coming down with more serious intent. The sky was already dark and threatening, but now the radio announced the storm had suddenly changed course and was moving directly towards shore.

She had been in her office, waiting on word from Daniel. The park was locked down and she had already sent everybody home. Clive had left with Jacobs and Palmer an hour ago. The last car she had spotted in the parking lot was Jerry's – she tapped up his number.

"Where are you? Why are you still here?"

"I'm still out on the grounds. Just doing a last walk-through."

"Seriously," Jen said. "Go home. Get safe. It looks like we're getting our weather early."

"I'll finish this last check," he said. "I'll lock-up if you want."

"No," Jen said. "You go. I'll stay on a little longer."

"Daniel's not back from the Grotto, yet?" he asked. "Sorry. Not my business. I couldn't help but overhear."

"Go home," Jen said. "Check-in mid-morning tomorrow. Plan on staying home."

"You need to talk?"

"Jerry. Go *home*."

"That an order, Chief?"

"That's an order," Jen replied.

She hung up, and then went to the window, watching until his car pulled out of the lot.

Jen obviously knew Jerry had eyes for her, but she was used to that – most men did. Although, as she was starting to get older, she had noticed a bit of a drop in that sort of attention – something that bothered her more than she thought it would.

She wondered if Jerry was baiting her – he'd certainly not mentioned Daniel by accident, and was more likely deliberately stoking the wound.

To be fair, besides asking her to dinner that one night, Jerry had never made any attempt to involve himself, but she also knew it wouldn't break his heart if things didn't work out with Daniel.

She wondered how his perspective might change if he knew she was pregnant.

Of course, she didn't even know what *Daniel's* reaction might be yet, either.

That was just one more reason Jen didn't like his little jaunt off to the Grotto today.

Jerry wasn't wrong when he'd picked-up on that little bit of angst. That was a seed that had already been long planted.

As the day started to stretch into afternoon, and the storm clouds began to billow like a smoking cauldron on the horizon, Jen found herself wondering what might be going on in the Grotto?

Somehow, she had allowed her estranged man, father of her child-to-be, to run off to a red-light district, to meet up with a skanky, swamp-tramp, with whom he already had a past.

Seriously, *how* did she manage to actually let that happen?

Daniel absolutely never talked about Abigail willingly – which, of course, only prodded Jen's insecurity all the more.

It wasn't for herself, exactly. Despite their recent problems, Jen knew Daniel loved her. Jen was as confident of that as ever. Daniel would kill or die for her.

But would he kill or die for Abigail as well?

There was chemistry there. Daniel wouldn't have said it at gunpoint, but Jen knew it all the same. And Daniel's feelings for Jen did not necessarily rule out feelings for Abigail as well – and *that* was the oldest story in the world.

Jen also knew he still thought about that night with her – out on the swamp, on a stormy night, just... like... *this*.

GOD, she hated that little bitch.

Jen checked her watch, glancing at the advancing progress of the clouds on the horizon.

The main front was definitely coming in early.

And Daniel had not yet returned from the Grotto – worrisome for more reason than one – those muddy back roads could be dangerous.

The storm would be coming from the east and wouldn't hit the western outskirts for about an hour, but there could still be flooding.

So where the hell *was* he?

Frustrated, she finally closed-up her office and made her way to her car, bracing as the rain and wind pushed at her like a physical force.

Water was already high on the roads as she pulled onto the highway, veering up the beach towards home.

The view afforded a good view of the coastal horizon – big, burly and angry clouds, dark and thundery, lit with neon-lightning.

She was ten miles into it when her phone beeped in her purse.

Jen glanced down, looking for a message from Daniel, but instead it was the park alert system.

She pulled over, logging into her work e-mail.

A security message popped up immediately – a fence was down, somewhere in the park. But when she attempted to access the security camera that had recorded the warning, she was unable.

Now the alarm stopped.

She frowned, indecisive.

Was it a glitch from the storm? Or was there really a fence down?

She sat there a moment on the side of the road, the wind and rain rocking her car.

A downed fence really shouldn't be an issue. Each enclosure was secured on its own. With the onset of the weather, it didn't seem likely that there had been a break-in. She thought about calling the police, but knew the storm would already be flooding their phone-lines long before the roads.

She checked her watch – twenty-minutes back.

With a sigh, Jen turned around. Better safe than sorry. It was her responsibility, and if she had to, she'd been stuck in the rain before.

On the other hand, this storm wasn't kidding around. The park was only a few blocks from the coast, and by the time she turned off the highway to the Gator Glades exit, the whole area was already getting the worst of it. Gutters were overflowing fast, and there was moving water on the streets.

As she pulled into the front lot, she saw the front gate was standing wide open.

Jerry's car was parked right in front of it.

Jen frowned as she pulled up beside it. Had he come back for some reason? Possibly tripped the alarm?

She stepped out into the rain, fighting through the wind over to the control booth for the main gate. She found the light on, and the drawers opened – likely rifled for keys.

Jen hit the button closing the front gate.

As the gated metal doors slid shut behind her, she stepped back out into the storm, making her way down the front walk back into the park.

When she passed the first of the snake houses, she saw all the doors were standing open. And when she looked inside, all of the cage doors had been sprung as well – thrown open, as if in a hurry.

She looked down at the water rushing by her feet, wondering if any of them had escaped already.

What was in this house? Central and South American vipers? The highly-venomous lance-heads known for sheer meanness. That was where they housed the Anacondas as well.

Jen stepped back, looking down the main mall of the park.

The exhibit doors had all been opened.

Did that mean the croc pens too?

As she stepped out onto the main road, she saw a figure in rain gear making his way over to Brutus' enclosure – the biggest saltie in the park.

"Hey!" Jen shouted over the wind.

Jerry turned.

When he saw it was her, he stopped.

"What in God's name are you *doing*?" Jen asked.

Jerry started walking towards her.

Jen held up her phone.

"I'm calling the police."

But even as she said it, she knew the emergency lines would be jammed.

"I'm sorry, Jen," Jerry said, reaching for her phone, knocking it out of her hand, "but I've got higher orders."

He was not, however, prepared for her response. He was only a middle-sized guy in the first place and, Daniel's offhand back-slap notwithstanding, it was not the first time a man had gotten physical with her.

She turned her hand out of his grip and doubled him over with a kick to the groin, followed by the heel of her palm to the nose. Blood spurted, and he grunted.

Blinking, off-balance, he started to come for her again, but was nearly knocked over by the wind. Jen felt the gust nearly threaten to pick her off her feet.

That was when the main storm surge came in.

Jen saw Jerry's eyes widen. She turned to see her own car riding the charging swell of water like a surfboard, crashing into Jerry's car, as the wave picked up both and burst through the front gate.

CHAPTER 15

The hybrid pond was closest to the entrance, facing the ocean, and the wave hit it first.

Both Jen and Jerry gaped as their cars smashed through the fences and the wave surged up and over the pond.

They tried to run, but the wave washed over them in moments.

Jen had the sense of immense weight suddenly forcing her down, like a house had been dropped on top of her. Then she was picked up and carried, and a moment later, she popped to the surface. Jerry came up sputtering beside her.

As they were swept along, they both looked around at the surrounding water and saw craggy backs being swept right along with them. Jen and Jerry exchanged wide-eyes.

Worse, the wave was washing them directly towards Brutus' enclosure – the biggest croc in the park – probably the biggest croc on the continent.

And pure saltie.

The spectator stands surrounding Brutus' pool were built with a roof. As they were carried past, Jen caught the corner.

Jerry reached out for her – Jen, after the slightest tick of hesitation, grabbed his hand, and they both clambered up onto the enclosure's roof, above the flooding wave.

They regarded each other warily as they clung to the rooftop, crouched on all fours, lest the wind knock them back into the fast-moving brine.

Jen looked out over the park.

All those open doors, open cages.

She turned to Jerry.

"*Why?*" she asked.

Jerry looked away.

"Because," he said, "we both work for Colin Mason. I'm just the only one that knew it." He shook his head regretfully. "For what it's worth, I didn't want this any more than you. But you learn to do what you're told."

Now he met her eye.

"You'll see."

Jen was about to publicly proclaim her resignation, when her car, which had been briefly hung-up on the fence to the hybrid pond, now broke loose and was swept directly into the shelter beneath their feet.

The support posts were broken and the roof collapsed into Brutus' pond.

Jen and Jerry were dumped in with it.

They clung to the structure as it collapsed, hanging on to the broken pillars as water now rushed over and past.

Jen had not spotted Brutus from the roof – he could have been carried away when the wave hit.

Or, he could have hunkered down at the bottom, as he had always done in the past during storms, riding out the rough weather, risking the surface only for brief breaths.

In which case, he could still be down there somewhere.

Around them, the remaining grandstands without their support-struts began to collapse inward, and the main dock began to fall along with it. Jen's car, still lodged where it had struck the shelter, broke loose again, careening into the remaining framework like a bumper boat.

The announcer's stand broke away.

With it, the fancy new croc cage, Gator Glades' most recent attraction, dropped into the pond.

A damn sight better, Jen thought, than hanging onto these loose pilings, waiting to see if Brutus was still around.

She glanced at Jerry, who nodded, and they both pushed away into the current, towards the floating cage.

They were ten feet away when Jerry was yanked beneath the surface.

Jen turned to see Brutus' scaly tail slap as the big croc turned in the water – Jerry was rolled briefly to the surface, gurgling out a strangled scream before being pulled back under.

For a moment, Jen reached reflexively to help, but the current was already pulling her away.

As if she could have done anything anyway.

She turned, paddling with all her strength for the cage.

The current nearly washed her past, but she caught hold, pulling herself over and on top.

She turned back to see Brutus almost on top of her.

Jen let out a scream, pulling the top open and falling inside, as the seventeen-foot croc smashed into the reinforced Plexiglas.

The jaws snapped at the open cage door, and Jen pulled it shut.

Brutus turned in the water, smacking the cage smartly with his tail – Jen felt an explosion of pain where her hand still clutched the door handle, jarring her whole arm to the shoulder with the impact – possibly breaking her wrist.

The big croc gave the cage two more solid slaps before turning away.

Brutus did not withdraw, however, but dropped below the surface, hovering just outside the cage, staring in – no doubt as he had done to many a tourist that had been teasingly dangled behind this solid clear barrier day after day.

After a moment, he came in again, bumping the transparent walls with his jaws.

Her wrist throbbing, Jen instinctively pulled back.

The big croc was clearly agitated by the storm – this was active territorial aggression. Jerry had been taken and then carelessly discarded, his body already washed away.

Brutus smacked the cage again.

Jen could feel the impact through the water. The cage was still attached to the collapsed pilings, but a few more strikes like that and the moorings might easily come loose.

That concern, however, quickly became secondary as Jen now realized Brutus' last blow had ruptured one of the pontoons that kept the cage afloat.

It was sinking.

CHAPTER 16

Daniel had been hightailing it, trying to reach the maintained roads before the rain hit. He didn't quite make it.

He had intended to meet Jen back at the park – there was no way he was going to have the post-Abigail conversation over the phone – especially not while trying to navigate these back-roads once the mud began to slide across, followed shortly by running water.

The parks truck was rough duty, but Daniel was still reduced to a crawl, as he made his way out of the marshlands into the city. By the time he reached the highway to the coast and Gator Glades, the storm had touched down with full force.

It was getting late and the park was another ten miles north. Daniel pulled out his phone – before he fought his way through the weather-front ahead, he better make sure Jen was still there.

Keep it brief, he thought, just tell her he was on his way – no details about Abigail until they were face-to-face.

Her number rang with no answer, before switching him to voicemail.

Daniel frowned. He pulled over, tapping out a text with an urgent beep.

She was probably on her way home, squirreling her car along through the weather, just like he was.

He waited for a response.

When there was none, he dialed Clive's number. Clive picked right up.

"Daniel? What's your story? You back yet?"

"I just hit the highway north. You get the park locked down okay?"

"Yeah," Clive replied, "Jen sent me and the two grunts home a couple hours ago."

"I just tried to call her."

"She was still at the park when I left." Clive hesitated briefly. "I think she was waiting on you."

Daniel glanced out the window – conditions were deteriorating quickly.

"You don't think she stayed, do you?

"She might have," Clive allowed.

"Hang on a second," Daniel said, putting the line on hold, and tapping the number for Jen's office. When that got no response, he tapped up a quick search for the Gator Glades' front office.

At the top of the search, his phone screen started playing a news bulletin – simultaneously, both his phone and the radio cut to the same feed – Ashley Wells reporting.

The image on Daniel's screen was the coastline ten miles north.

"This is Ashley Wells," the phone and radio announced together, "approximately ten minutes ago, a Tsunami wave was reported along the southeastern coast of Florida, causing massive flooding."

The screen shifted to images of people in boats around their houses, still pulling other people out of the water. Ashley Wells was reporting from the highway ramp above.

Gator Glades would be another two miles north – right at the brunt of it.

Daniel switched back to Clive.

"Are you seeing this? Turn on your TV."

"Hold on," Clive said.

After a moment, he came back on.

"Jesus," he said.

"Do you think Jen was still at the park?" Daniel asked.

"I'll meet you there," Clive said, and hung up.

Daniel pulled back onto the road, stepping on the gas with more urgency now.

Clive lived five miles north, and was already waiting where the road going further on was now underwater. He had brought his pick-up with his own fishing boat in tow.

He waved at Daniel as he pulled up.

"Figured we were gonna need this," Clive shouted over the wind.

He unhooked the boat, and rolled the trailer into the water. The two men clambered aboard, and Clive cranked the old outboard up, motoring them out into the fast-moving water towards Gator Glades.

In a way, the location where the wave had hit was lucky – the entire area bordered on protected lands, and so there weren't that many people, and any residences lay at the perimeter.

For Gator Glades, however, it was about as bad as it could get.

As they approached the park, the first thing they saw was the front gates standing open, seemingly knocked ajar, as six-feet of water flooded the park beyond.

Daniel and Clive exchanged wide-eyes as Clive steered them through.

The hybrid pond was completely flooded over.

"Well," Clive said. "That's our whole summer's work right there." He glanced out at the surrounding water. "Probably swimming around us right now."

"It's more than that," Daniel said. "Look."

The waterline was up past the windows for most buildings on the lot, but they could see the doors to the animal enclosures standing open.

"It's all of them," Daniel said. "What the hell happened here?"

He looked around at the murky water. Clive was right – there were probably two-hundred crocodiles, not to mention gators, snakes, and lizards of all kinds, schooling all around them.

Some of them, Daniel thought, as the wind and rain rocked their boat, probably still had pieces of Alex Kintner digesting in their guts.

"Daniel," Clive said, "look."

Daniel turned to where Clive was pointing at the smashed and sunken grandstands leading to Brutus' enclosure.

Jen's car was wedged into the wreckage.

Clive glanced at Daniel grimly, cranking the motor.

Daniel's heart hammered in his chest.

What was he about to see?

Something like that little girl – her disembodied head and arm?

Her dead, bloodless skin?

Or the third of a corpse that was left of Alex, barely two days ago?

Clive steered them around the wreckage.

Jen's car was empty.

Daniel shut his eyes.

Then Clive spoke up.

"I think I've found your lady," he said.

Daniel's heart skipped a beat when he saw Clive pointing out into the middle of Brutus' pond.

Then he saw the croc cage floating ajar at the surface, still tethered to the half-sunk wreckage of the podium.

He could see Jen inside, waving frantically at them through the reinforced Plexiglas.

The moment of cool relief, however, was followed immediately by cold new peril as Daniel now saw that one of the cage's floats had burst and dropped below the surface, leaving the other barely holding the cage above water. Jen had a small space for air.

"Jen!" Daniel shouted over the wind. "Are you okay?"

Her voice was muffled, and nearly drowned out.

"Not for long! This thing is sinking!"

"We're going to try and get to you!"

"Be careful!" she shouted back. "Brutus is still in here!"

That proved to be a timely warning as Clive started to take them past the half-sunken, and totally demolished gate into the enclosure – Brutus was waiting for them.

There was a huge jolt, and the big croc's massive tail swept over the side, even as the tooth-studded jaws curled back, gaping and ready.

Both men ducked the sweeping tail – it was a move crocs were known for – using their tails to swat prey directly into their mouths. Brutus did it pretty well, too – a half-second difference with no warning, and he would have gotten at least one of them.

Clive gunned the motor as the big croc now lunged up over the side of the boat with his jaws.

But the boat lurched forward, and Brutus dropped back in the water.

Daniel blinked. For a split-second, the jaws had been within a foot of his face – he had felt the displaced air and heard the shotgun-snap as the teeth crashed together.

Clive gave Brutus some distance, but the big croc was already moving after them. Clive pulled back steadily.

"Jesus, he's being aggressive," Clive said respectfully. "He's guarding that territory hard. There's no way he's going to let us across."

He glanced at Daniel.

"You didn't happen to bring a rifle, did you?"

"I've got my service pistol," Daniel said. "But I wouldn't put it against that thick hide. Not without a perfect shot."

"And that big old croc isn't going to give us a perfect shot," Clive agreed.

Jen's cap of air had already grown smaller. Within minutes, the top of the cage would be underwater, but Brutus wasn't going to let them near it.

Daniel looked around at the suddenly-prehistoric waters, wondering how many other crocs were also circling around them, just waiting for that moment of inattention.

And rising up out of the Jurassic swamp was the brontosaurus-shadow of the parked crane, looming over the hybrid pond.

"Clive," Daniel asked, "can you drive that?"

Clive eyeballed the water depth. It had receded somewhat from the initial ten-foot wave, down to around five or six-feet.

"I can drive it," he said. "I just hope I can get it across the lot."

He steered them over, grabbing hold of the big rig's wheel, which was just at the water line. He hiked up onto the wheel, climbing into the operator's seat.

There was a dinosaurian rumble as Clive turned the engine on.

The giant brontosaur-image was complete as the massive rig began to roll forward ponderously, plowing the water as it rolled across the lot.

Daniel puttered the boat along beside.

Clive rolled the crane up to the edge of the wrecked grandstands. There was a mechanical snort as he shifted to a stop, followed by a hydraulic grunt as the long neck reached over the top, stretching out over the water. Clive maneuvered the giant arm over the floating croc cage and lowered the grappling hook.

Daniel could see Jen pulling away as the heavy metal hook bumped the top of the cage, looking for purchase.

Her space of air was almost gone now.

Deftly, Clive threaded the crane-hook through the cage's own moorings. He reversed the cable, cinching up the hook, and the cage bobbed upright.

The Plexiglas cylinder began to rise up out of the water.

And as it started to pull away – to *retreat* – Brutus attacked.

Three-quarters of a ton worth of crocodile leaped up out of the water – the neck of the crane jolted as the creature's full weight came down on top of the cage.

The jaws latched onto the cable itself, clinging doggedly.

Clive kept bringing the cage up and now he was pulling the big croc out of the water with it.

Brutus began to thrash, rocking the crane, knocking the cage around roughly, threatening to jar it loose from the cable or, worse, break the moorings completely away.

Daniel saw Jen's head knocked against the Plexiglas, backed with the impact of Brutus' estimated sixteen-hundred pounds of body weight.

Jen fell limp, floating inside the cage.

Daniel cursed aloud, drawing his service pistol and opening fire, aiming for the back of the beast's head, the only viable kill-shot with a big croc. He fired several shots in succession, all hitting the big thrashing target, but nowhere near the skull, instead bouncing off the plated back.

They obviously hurt, though – Brutus bellowed, releasing his grip, spinning off the top of the cage, thrashing quickly into the water and out of sight.

"You get him?" Clive hollered down.

"Oh, I got him," Daniel shouted back. "I didn't kill him, but I'm pretty sure I pissed him off."

Clive cranked the cable, pulling the cage clear of the water, turning the crane's neck back out of the enclosure, pulling the rig away from Brutus' pen.

If the big croc's territorial instincts were in hyper-drive because of the storm, hopefully he'd stay to defend his own pond, rather than follow them out.

Hopefully.

Clive lowered the cage down beside the boat.

Jen was lying unconscious inside. Daniel climbed on top, pulling open the door and clambering in beside her.

She had a nasty cut on her scalp, but she was breathing on her own. Scooping her up, Daniel scrambled back out of the cage, climbing back down into the boat as Clive jumped down out of the crane's operator's seat.

Daniel had his phone out as Clive revved the boat motor.

"I'm calling for an emergency chopper," Daniel said, nodding meaningfully to Clive. "Let's see if we can beat them to the hospital."

Clive kicked up a plume of water, as he turned the boat and steered them back out the main gates.

Daniel glanced back over his shoulder at the flooded park.

He wondered how many – crocs, snakes, lizards – all the deadliest on Earth. They would have to contact the police, fire-department, any first-responders, and warn them to be wary.

And, he thought with a sigh, they better inform the press as well. The public had a right to know what had just been let loose in their backyards.

In his lap, Jen stirred, moaning softly.

"Easy," Daniel whispered, holding her still, shielding her as best he could from the still-pouring rain.

Clive revved the motor as they left Gator Glades behind.

And in their wake, sporting two fresh bullet wounds on his less-armored side and legs, Brutus popped to the surface.

His home had been invaded – despoiled. It was tainted to him now. He no longer felt safe here.

The big croc's scaly back floated among the debris, letting the current carry him out of the enclosure that had been his dwelling for more than twenty years, out into the open Everglades beyond.

CHAPTER 17

"It's good to see you, Abigail," Colin Mason said. "I've been looking for you for a long time."

He was sitting at her father's old desk, tapping away, bathed in the computer screen's electric blue light. He smiled as he turned to her.

"I've been looking through some of your father's old videos." He nodded over his shoulder to the now-closed doorway leading to the croc-pit below.

"It was just as easy to open them up here," Mason said, "rather than down in that smelly hole."

He tapped the keyboard, switching over to a live-bulletin – coverage of the storm surge that had flooded nearly five miles of coastline.

Mason smiled each time Ashley Wells' grave, concerned face appeared on-screen.

"I *like* her," he said.

Abigail said nothing. If she had only brought her damned rifle. She glanced over her shoulder, gauging whether she could get out the back door, around the house to her truck – or perhaps through the front door – Mason only had one leg. He didn't appear to be carrying a gun.

But something in his eye held her in place.

"I take it you know who I am?" Mason asked gently.

Abigail nodded.

Mason turned back to the screen.

"Right now," he said, "I am rerouting this whole security-feed to my own personal network. Anything recorded here will now go directly to me. I've already got over four years of footage."

He smiled broadly.

"Some of it," he said, "is pretty good."

Abigail resisted the urge to shut her eyes – at least now she didn't have to wonder – if the record of her life hadn't gone beyond Ol' Bill's personal PC before, it had now.

Mason tapped to a different screen – this one the menu for the security cameras. At least two-dozen views popped up, all from different cameras posted all over the property. Mason tapped through until the image on-screen was inside the cabin itself.

Abigail could see herself from all four walls, and four different angles, yet had not yet spotted a single visible camera.

"This," Mason said, "is recording right now. Where the motion is."

His grin broadened.

"And the night's just getting started."

Mason turned his full attention to her now.

"I've never been to this cabin before," he said. "But all the black-market routes to the south coast go back to the Pirates of the Caribbean days."

He smiled.

"Of course," he continued, "I can be arrested just for being on American soil." He shrugged. "But that's the sort of thing that adds zest, isn't it?"

Abigail nodded noncommittally.

She thought she understood Mason well enough.

Despite his methodical, old-tomcat-style, his urges were what drove him.

When they were activated, they stepped into dominance, and the rest of the personality, the step-by-step gamesman, was all there just to enable and cover for these indulgences.

Abigail had seen that sort of thing before.

She had even been accused of it.

In Mason's eyes, she recognized that unmistakable glint of the appetite starting to grow out of control.

As he stared at Abigail, bathed in electric blue, there was hunger in his eyes.

Abigail only wondered what appetites had been aroused.

Mason leaned forward in his chair – once her father's chair – now probably Daniel's.

His smile grew long-suffering. He looked at her gravely.

"You," he said, "have a lot to answer for."

He shook his head, like a father adding up the tally on his daughter's credit card.

"You disrupted an entire operation," Mason said. "Everything from production to distribution. And you 'touched' someone who, by association, should have been untouchable."

Abigail shrugged.

Mason held up an admonishing finger.

"Ordinarily," he said, "there's only one answer for any one of the above, let alone all of them."

But now he tapped the reproachful finger on the desk.

"You, however," he said, "are Ol' Bill's daughter."

Mason shrugged.

"Your father and I go way back," he said. "He was first brought to my attention after one of my employees on the distributing side, working out of the Everglades, had gone missing. And the general consensus was that your father had something to do with it.

"It turned out," Mason continued, "that, hell yeah, he did. My operatives found it on video-tape. They sent me a copy."

Mason smiled.

"Your father was already a valuable asset on the production side. He would have been hard to replace on the water. I would have been loath to lose him.

"But," he said, "it turned out we also had common interests."

Mason shrugged.

"From that point forward," he said, "we... collaborated."

He held up his cautionary finger

"We never met. I was careful about that. But we became like pen-pals that shared home movies."

Mason smiled.

"Sharks were always my passion. But I've always really *liked* crocodiles."

"Yeah," Abigail said quietly. "So did my father. I can see where you two would have gotten along."

"I've known you, as well," Mason replied. "Ever since you fed young Johnny Marvin to big Caesar." He smiled. "Four years old and cute as a button. I've got it on VHS and DVD."

He eyed her.

"And like I said, you've grown up nice. I've paid attention. I own most of the higher-end gentleman's clubs along the south coast. You've worked for me when you didn't even know it. Ever since you ran away, I looked after you. I let your father know you were fine."

Mason leaned forward.

"I even stopped in and caught your show once or twice. You were an eye-catcher. But out of respect for your father, I never touched you. Otherwise, I might have... *cultivated* you myself."

Now he eyed her speculatively.

"Of course," he said, "he's gone now. And you *have* put yourself in this position."

Abigail looked into Mason's eyes and recognized the predator.

A one-legged man, getting on in years – ordinarily she wouldn't even have blinked.

She would have put the knife in her belt to his throat. She would have kicked his twitching corpse into the gator pond.

Instead, she made a break for the door.

Mason, on his one leg, somehow got there before she did, intercepting her with his massive frame.

He caught her arm. The strength of his hands was... *terrifying* – like the jaws of a croc.

But his eyes were worse. Abigail had seen the glowing eyes of crocs and gators all her life – some of them just had that look – like they just *wanted* you.

This was the look of one who *had* you.

They stood like that for a moment. Abigail waited to see if he would wrench her arm, perhaps break it, maybe throw her to the floor.

Instead, he smiled.

Almost gently, he pulled her back to his chair, now sitting her on his one knee. He tapped the keyboard.

"Here," he said. "Watch."

The screen blinked to the image of Abigail at four years old – waddling to the edge of the deck with a human arm in her hand.

Abigail tensed in Mason's lap, his one hand holding her in place tightened just a little.

He made her sit through the whole thing.

Then the next one – two weeks before her sweet-sixteen, feeding Virgil to Caesar and Nemo.

Abigail tried to shut her eyes, but Mason gave her a stiff shake.

The video with Pete came on next.

She was an adult woman this time, grown into a predator in her own right.

"What do you want from me?" Abigail asked.

Mason turned her on his knee to face him.

Then the hand on her arm released and he allowed her to stand.

He tapped onto the next screen.

This was the video of her night with Daniel.

Mason turned down the sound, and turned on some background music – slow, reedy, heartbeat rhythm.

He settled back in his chair, a very grizzled old tom.

"I want you to dance for me," he said.

He pulled out his own phone, and propped it up on the desk. He turned the camera onto record.

"I'm sure the security cameras are recording this anyway, but I want my own copy."

He smiled.

Abigail stared back balefully.

How many nights had she looked into the eyes of some drunken lout paying her singles and twenties to grind in his lap?

She glanced at the video playing – four screens' worth – from Daniel carrying her across the threshold, lit by the strobing flash of lightning, and then into the bedroom under electric computer-screen blue – all alone out in the primeval swamp, on a raging, stormy night, just like this one.

All set to music.

Abigail began to dance.

Swaying with the steady beat, she shut her eyes, letting her body act on its own, just like she'd done on stage – separating from the audience leering back, some rapt, some smoldering, some loud, hooting and rowdy.

It hadn't been that long after all.

Mason smiled as she leaned over him, letting her hair fall over his shoulders, brushing her chest close to his face.

She sat back in his lap, slicing over his one knee, pulling herself close.

With the speed of a viper, she pulled the knife from her belt and brought it to his throat, aiming for the jugular.

She heard him laugh as he snatched her hand, folding the knife away from her like a little child.

"I was *waiting* for that one," he chuckled amiably.

Then he grabbed her.

She felt herself picked up, as he rose on his single leg, loping into the bedroom and throwing her onto the bed.

Now Abigail began to fight – which, of course, was exactly what he wanted.

He seemed to be made of steel. And for the first time since she was fifteen, ever since she'd left this cabin more than twenty years ago, Abigail found herself completely and utterly helpless.

She screamed in outrage.

Her cries echoed out over the swamp.

And all around, the cameras were recording.

CHAPTER 18

Hours later, Abigail lay in bed.

In the aftermath, she felt violated and filthy. She hadn't believed she could ever be *taken* again.

She stopped struggling fairly early on – which was different than submitting. After all, she had bartered for her feminine-wares before.

Tammy had also taught her it was perfectly acceptable to submit to force if it got you close enough to cut his throat.

But in the end, that hadn't mattered either.

And eventually, she did submit after all.

There wasn't a bruise on her, and perhaps that was her deepest shame – she couldn't even force him to hurt her.

Mason was in the shower – another upgrade since the time she'd lived here. Back in the old days, it was a hand-pump out of the river.

The steam filled the room and reflected the pulse of lightning from the still-raging storm.

Mason had left the door open – just as vulnerable and unsuspecting as he could be.

Abigail wasn't fooled. She knew he was *never* unsuspecting.

What he was doing was *daring* her.

But if she didn't rise to it, she was as much as surrendering.

She had fancied herself the black widow. But even a venomous spider was just a snack to a carnivorous lizard.

Still, she buoyed herself by remembering this was nothing that had never happened to her before.

There was no need to become unglued – no need to be baited into rash action.

No need to do anything other than what she'd come to do in the first place.

Moving quietly, she slipped out of bed, retrieving her clothes where they had been tossed to the floor, and dressed quickly.

She found her knife still lying where Mason had carelessly tossed it.

Abigail slipped it in her back pocket, glancing over her shoulder. Mason was humming a tune in the shower, showing no sign he was aware of her movements.

The parks department had done very little renovation. Apart from a file cabinet or two, most of the rest of the cabin was as Ol' Bill left it – including his supply closet, which was always well-stocked in the most basic traditional back-ups – first and foremost, the ability to start a fire.

It was raining hard, but enough kerosene spread around, and the place would burn from the inside out.

The building wasn't that big, and Ol' Bill was well-supplied – in a matter of moments, Abigail had poured oil all over the cabin.

She was about to light the match when suddenly Mason was there.

Abigail screamed.

Mason grabbed her hand, and for a moment she was frozen.

She had thought she had no fear left in her – she had stared-down a twenty-foot crocodile and not blinked.

But something about this man's eyes made her fail.

She fought anyway, kicking at his leg.

He was ready for it. His knee should have bent but instead the joint held firm. It was like kicking a tree. But it did cause him to let go of her briefly. Now he reached for her again.

This time, instead of fighting, Abigail lit the match and threw it to where the kerosene pooled on the floor at their feet.

She felt the blast of air before the heat as the flame ignited.

The entire cabin lit-up at once.

Mason was caught by surprise and reflexively shielded his face against the sudden flame. Abigail took the opportunity to kick at his leg again. This time he was off balance and stumbled back.

Abigail ran for the back door, the flames licking after her bare legs and singeing her hair. The door was hanging open where Mason had kicked it in, and she wrenched it shut behind her.

The deadbolt had been knocked away cleanly but Abigail jammed her knife into the socket, wedging it into the empty space. It wouldn't stop Mason, but in a burning building with a door that opened inward, it might slow him down enough – especially, if he didn't realize immediately what was holding the kicked-in door shut.

For good measure, she shoved the table on the back porch in front of the doorway.

As she stepped into the storm, the crash of the rain hit her like a physical weight. It was like trying to swim upstream as she circled around to the front.

The cabin burned from the inside like a jack-o-lantern.

Abigail could see Mason through the front window – he was smiling at her through the flames.

He was enjoying himself – enjoying the chase.

Well then, Abigail thought, let's give him his money's worth.

She ran to her truck. She glanced briefly at her rifle, but instead pulled out the three containers of gasoline she'd brought just for this purpose. and pitched them one after the other into the flame.

Then she jumped into her truck, cranked the engine, spinning wheels in the mud, as she skidded out the main drive.

Behind her, there was a loud boom as the first of the gas containers lit. Then two more immediately followed.

Abigail hoped Mason had gotten a good look at it.

The rain continued to come down in a torrent, and the surrounding swamp was encroaching on the narrow road.

Out on the water, the scattered land-banks were rapidly disappearing.

Abigail had no doubt the gator pond had flooded as well – maybe not overflowing – her father built for weather – but that's what the gate was for.

And Mason had opened the gate.

The whole surrounding area was already saturated with dangerous invasive species. Now a congested pool of hybrid and invasive crocodiles had just been released.

Which meant that the waters around the cabin had now become the most dangerous in the world.

A mile past the cabin was where the road crossed the fork in the river. The water below was nearly up to the bridge. The route had been cut through the swamp across as much of the highlands as possible – often at five-feet or less above sea-level – sometimes a *lot* less. It was impassible during the rainy season, and you could only access the cabin by boat.

Because, while the bridge remained, the roads on both sides had a tendency to flood over – as they were now.

To be fair to the county, the only one who would have cared was Ol' Bill, and he didn't care at all – the fewer visitors the better.

Having no choice, she tried to take the truck through. The water was two-feet deep leading up to the bridge, and at least that deep on the opposite side of the swelling river – but her rig was large, and if she could get another mile up the road, the elevation went up around the bend.

Her tires maintained traction as the truck plowed through the running water. There was a thump as they reached the wooden planks of the bridge.

She was just thinking she was going to make it, when her engine sputtered and died.

Abigail smacked the wheel, cursing. She glanced over her shoulder – she'd gone maybe thirty yards down the flooded road – two feet of water all the way back.

Just two feet, but that could hide a hundred crocs, and there could be easily that many out here right now, depending on how full that pond had been.

The fork in the river cut off this last major land-base from the rest of the highlands – beyond the bridge was her father's cabin and nothing else.

Except...

Abigail glanced up the river where it veered northwest – the fork branched off in several directions, but the main channel rejoined the river on the other side. Abigail knew the waterways like the back of her hand.

This was Ol' Bill's swamp – and her playground growing up.

It had been a long time, but technical upgrades aside, her father was a creature of habits – and pretty much everything was still where he left it.

Now she had a destination in mind.

Abigail took a breath, shutting her eyes.

When she opened them, she was calm.

High-living had not made her soft – she was a creature of the swamp as much as any gator. And if she had to, she could fight for territory with the best of them.

She retrieved her rifle from the back seat.

Moving slowly, letting the pounding rain camouflage her movements, Abigail stepped out of the truck into the storm.

She slung her rifle over one shoulder, aimed and ready, as she waded through the running water.

CHAPTER 19

There were nights on the water like this when Abigail was a kid – nights when her father wasn't... safe... to be around.

He'd be 'gettin' into his cups', and there would be that wobble in his leg, and then after that, he'd get mean. He didn't always, but Abigail had learned to watch for it the way a deer watches for movement at the water hole.

On these nights, she mostly had a boat, but that was only after it became regular enough that she'd developed a routine.

But not on those first few nights she hadn't – she'd just run into the dark and hid out the night in the surrounding swamp, crouched in the bushes, in the pitch blackness of the swamp, with fireflies, screeching birds, slithering snakes, and even flapping bats – the Everglades had every box checked when it came to terrifying sights or sounds if you were a little girl hiding from your drunken father out on the water.

And of course, there was the deep-throated guttural bellows of gators.

That was the difference back then – it was all alligators – there were only a few crocs in the area – and precious damn few cobras, black mambas, or pythons.

All of which had been stocked in numbers within a five-to-ten mile area, and the immediate square mile in particular.

Abigail had to remind herself that this wasn't the swamp she'd grown up in – the rules had changed.

She made her way carefully back up the flooded road, her rifle poised, as she waded through the thigh-deep water. She could feel the river debris bouncing off her legs in the fast moving current, and kept her finger poised on the trigger, lest one of those passing objects suddenly turn and bite.

But she got to the muddy road without incident.

Then she headed up the north fork through the brush.

She was barefoot, but her feet were toughened nearly to the point of cloven hooves from an early lifetime without shoes. She slogged her way through the thick wild brush.

At one point, a large snake slithered across the path in front of her.

It had turned at her approach, and in the dark, Abigail couldn't tell if it was a small python, or perhaps a large viper – or even a cobra or Taipan – they were all out there.

All she could see was the slender shape poised, suddenly facing her in the dark, and the hissing whisper as it hovered briefly within striking range.

Abigail froze.

But the snake, whatever it was, was apparently content to retreat without further trouble. It dropped the striking pose and disappeared into the brush.

Abigail waited motionless for several minutes, making sure it had gone, letting the rain wash over her like part of the foliage.

How far through to the other side? Three miles, maybe – out where the channel branched back into the main river?

It all surrounded the mini-island that had been her father's property.

On the west shore, opposite the cabin, her father kept an old fishing shack, and he usually had a boat docked.

Of course, she hadn't been there in more than twenty years.

It was still dark when she made her way to the river.

The storm was finally losing strength. There remained the rattle of thunder and wind, but the main front was now moving north.

Abigail had no idea of the time – Mason had kept at her for... *hours*. When she had fled the cabin, it was well after midnight.

The continued gusts of rain filtered her view like fog as she searched the waterline for the old shack.

Finally, she spotted the square shape in the dark, rising up out of the water, mounted on stilts.

She felt a rush of relief when she saw the small boat tethered on the small dock built alongside.

Unfortunately, with the flooded waters, the shack itself was twenty yards out into the flowing river.

Abigail looked out on the water. She could see nothing but darkness, wind and rain.

The crocs were there. She knew it. Probably hunkering down near the bottom, waiting out the storm.

That could work to her advantage – as would the pounding rain at the surface, hiding the ripples of her own movements.

If she moved slowly, she was just another floating log.

She grabbed-up a broken branch and poked it out in the water just off the bank. Nothing bit it. Hopefully, the crocs would be keeping to the deeper waters further out. They *should*.

Abigail took a breath, steeling herself.

Then, with her rifle aimed and ready, she waded into the water.

The current tugged at her feet and she again felt the touch of debris going by. In only a few steps she was at waist depth.

She looked out at the shack, barely fifteen yards away.

But depending on what might be waiting down below, that was a big fifteen.

She shouldered her rifle, stepping into the deeper water and started swimming.

Now, she was moving like prey, swimming near the surface, fighting the current – no longer a floating log.

Bits of swamp scrap bounced off of her arms – every touch sent a dose of adrenaline into her veins. She did her best to keep her movements slow and deliberate, but the current threatened to pull her past the shack.

With something like terror, even as the thunder and lightning crashed above, she broke out into an open swim, stroking and kicking, in a bolt to the shack.

She latched one hand on the deck. As she did so, she felt something brush her leg. She never saw what it was before she hauled herself up out of the water, scurrying away from the edge, pressing up against the wooden walls of the shack.

It was a small structure – inside, it measured less than ten-by-ten feet. It was thirty years old and likely had not been used since Ol' Bill had died. Tucked into the little cove, clear on the opposite side of the island, the parks department probably didn't even know it was there.

Abigail pushed open the door, pulling a string dangling from the ceiling. She smiled when the light came on.

"Still works," she said aloud. "Good old Daddy."

The interior was a storage house of traps and rods, nets and lines – all of it remarkably orderly, clean and handy. She rooted around until she found a flashlight. She clicked it on and pulled the drawstring dark again, stepping back out onto the dock.

Abigail appraised the rickety old rowboat tied to the little dock, and measured it against the still-active storm.

Going against the current in *this* with nothing but oars wasn't an option. Fortunately, she didn't need to.

Further downstream led to the lagoon surrounding the Hanging Tree.

She grabbed-up a couple of gaffs and ropes, and tossed them into the little boat before she stepped in herself, and pushed off into the current.

With her rifle ready at her feet, she began to row, turning out into the deepest part of the river, letting the water carry her along like a leaf on the surface, quickly past any crocs lurking below. That just left her to avoid obstacles – she bumped off multiple trees and floating logs in the dark.

There was also a stretch of the river where the overhanging branches reached down like claws, almost to the waterline. When the river ran high, if it was passable at all, you could easily get tangled and trapped and drown.

Passing through was like being dragged through a briar patch.

She made it to the Hanging Tree a little before dawn.

Somewhere during that time, the storm finally stopped.

And now that the weather had blown over, the crocs were there.

The lagoon that surrounded the tree was full of blinking eyes. Abigail shined her light and the surface was a mob of beady jack-o-lanterns. There had already been crocs congested in this area, but the current went this way from the cabin and the area was a natural catch-basin – a lot of the crocs Mason had released just last night would have ended up here too.

Abigail regarded her rickety boat, measured against some of the scaly backs she saw floating between her and the tree. Most of them were smallish, but there were several she estimated over ten-feet.

A few were larger than that.

With her rifle ready, she began to row.

She felt a couple of experimental bumps from below, but most of the floating eyes parted as the little boat – which was still larger than they were – made its way past.

Crocs were pretty simple in their hierarchy. The biggest got his way. So even a fourteen-foot rowboat had bluff potential.

The thing about crocs, though, was the bigger they were, meant the older they were, and by the time they got big enough to take on a boat, they also knew what it was.

Abigail was within fifteen feet of the Hanging Tree when a big one finally zeroed in on her.

She saw it at the last minute as its back raised up beside her, rocking the boat, nearly capsizing it, even as the massive tail swept over the side. Abigail threw herself forward, but the tail clipped her forearm – it was like being snagged by a car-bumper going at speed. Pain lanced through her arm and wrist and she realized the blow had broken her right wrist, just above the hand.

Abigail grabbed-up her rife – her left being her dumb hand – and fired a blast into the water, but the big croc had already dropped back below the surface.

The other eyes, however, were encroaching quickly.

And as she looked down, she realized that her feet were now in ankle-deep water. The floorboards had been cracked and the boat was sinking.

Wincing, holding her injured arm tucked at her side, Abigail reached for the rope still dangling from the overhead branch of the Hanging Tree.

The end of the rope was torn and bloody.

Abigail pulled herself over to the trunk of the tree where she had left Cross' phone. She found it still nestled in the little carved-out notch – probably still filming. She hoped it still had a charge going.

There was a sudden lurch as the boat was again struck from below, and now the leak broke open and water began seeping in. Abigail saw the snapping jaws reaching over the side and she pulled back quickly. She felt the jaw-snap splash droplets of water in her face.

She snatched Cross' phone out of its notch, even as she tossed her rifle over her shoulder, and hiked herself up into the split in the trunk of the Hanging Tree, monkeying her way up onto the main overhanging branch.

With her back against the trunk, she leaned the barrel of her rifle across one knee, guiding it with her left hand, aiming it down on the water below.

The first rays of dawn had started to creep.

There was no sunrise in the swamp, but there was suddenly ambient light, and she realized she could see.

In the calm aftermath of the storm, the water below was a flat as gelatin.

With the explosion of her rifle shots, most of the beady eyes had disappeared from the surface.

But the crocs were still there.

Abigail held her rifle ready, looking for that big bastard – at least a fourteen-footer.

She only had the bullets left in the chamber, but if she could kill a couple of them, crocs were fast learners, and the others would keep their distance.

The first scaly back that finally popped back to the surface, Abigail shot it in the sweet spot behind the eye. The croc, a ten-footer, kicked and disappeared. Abigail was pretty sure she hit the target, but you never knew when you shot them in the water – that was why you typically got them on the beach.

Surprisingly, it was only a few minutes before more craggy backs appeared at the surface.

The other crocs had scattered, but only briefly. They were bold around the tree.

They had, after all, been fed here recently.

Abigail supposed she only had herself to blame for that one.

She shot two more of them. The others finally gave distance.

For now.

Abigail had not called for help many times in her life. There would have been no point – there would have been no one to come.

Ironic the way some things had changed.

She tapped Cross' phone, bringing up the dwindling screen, and entered Daniel's number.

CHAPTER 20

The coast remained flooded for nearly a five-mile stretch – the storm had blown over, but the wave surge flooded a lot of the lowlands before it receded, and left a lot of standing water.

Some of that water had teeth.

The first croc attack that day was at barely six a.m.

A man had taken a canoe around the flooded neighborhood – his phone, which was found in the empty boat, showed him panning across the surrounding houses, some with the water-levels up past their porches. It also showed him spotting a craggy back, and he could be heard talking into the speaker, assuming it was a big alligator, and he actually came in closer for a better look.

As it turned out, it was Brutus, already cranky after the incident at the park, and the big croc had reared up and snatched him right out of the canoe.

No one actually saw this attack, and the man didn't get reported missing until he failed to show up at work two days later.

But he was far from the only story.

Despite early reports and warning bulletins, in the flooded areas, as people began to emerge, picking-up after the storm, some in boats, some wading in the hip-deep water, four people were taken by crocs before word got around to stay clear of the water.

First responders, however, had no choice – FEMA had anticipated the storm, despite its early arrival, and aid-units were already on the scene at some of the worst-hit areas – by seven a.m., two rescue workers had been hit by crocs, accounting for one fatality.

Nor was every incident restricted to the flooded areas. One man had his leg broken simply walking out to his car, and failing to see the seven-foot croc that had wandered up out of the water and taken refuge under his car. The scaly tail had swept him off his feet, fracturing his shin, and leaving him staring at a hissing mouthful of teeth.

The man had scrambled away, limped back into the house to call 911, and found the line busy.

It wasn't just crocs either.

An old woman called about a lizard eating her cat – which was something that actually happened a lot in modern Florida, with rampant Nile monitors and tegu lizards. On this occasion, however, police discovered a nine-foot Komodo dragon waiting for them in the woman's back yard.

The giant lizard had viciously bitten one of the officers before retreating into the canal behind the house after the second officer took a shot at it – the small caliber pistol fire, however, ricocheted off the dragon's deceptively well-armored back.

Someone also caught footage of Buffy, Gator Glades' world-record-class reticulated python as it lounged, hanging from the low-hanging branch of a flooded tree. The clip would make Ashley Wells' morning broadcast, accompanied by the first reports of attacks all over the area as the full-impact of what had happened at the reptile park became apparent.

Brutus retreated from the area fairly early on.

The big croc had huddled to the bottom after taking the canoer, the man's limp form still clutched in his jaws. But then choppers began to arrive, accompanied by more, and larger boats.

Brutus had been in captivity for a long time, but he had been wild-born.

Now that he was out of his cage, his first instinct was to get as far away as he could from humans.

The big croc turned and headed deeper into the glades.

CHAPTER 21

Daniel was sleeping fitfully across two chairs in the hospital waiting room when he was woken by a doctor.

"Ranger Reid? She's awake. She's been asking to see you."

Daniel sat up painfully. The sun was just shining its first light in the windows. He had sent Clive home last night.

"Get some rest," he told him. "Tomorrow's going to be a busy day. I'll stay on here."

Now, wiping sleep out of his eyes, Daniel checked his phone, thinking that Clive was probably already out at the park station with Jacobs and Palmer.

Sure enough, he saw a message: "Already starting to get calls. How's Jen?"

Daniel followed the doctor into Jen's room to find her sitting up in bed, watching the news

Ashley Wells was on the air early today, her grave, concerned face intoning the list of casualties from the storm, even as a new tally began to mount.

"They've already reported four crocodile attacks," Jen said, looking up as Daniel entered the room and sat down by her bed. "They've also brought up Gator Glades ten times, but they haven't mentioned me yet."

"I didn't tell them that part," Daniel said.

He glanced at the doctor, who nodded.

"I'll give you two a few minutes." he said, and stepped out.

Jen's head was bandaged – a pretty good thump on the noggin' according to the doctor, and her right wrist had been wrapped in a splint – cracked, not broken. They'd given her a sedative, and she'd slept most of the night.

"How are you feeling?" Daniel asked.

"A little banged-up and sore," she said, waving it off. "I'll be alright."

She looked back up at the TV.

"It was Jerry," she said. "He was a Colin Mason-toadie. He opened the pens. Everything that could get out is out. Every last gator, every last Komodo lizard, viper, cobra or python. Buffy's out there somewhere."

She sighed.

"And an entire pond-full of hybrid crocodiles. A hundred and fifty animals there alone."

Daniel nodded slowly. He pulled out his phone and tapped Clive's number.

"Hey, Chief," Clive responded. "How's your lady?"

Daniel glanced at Jen – he knew this time the reference was for her.

"She's on the mend," he said. "I got your message. You're already getting calls?"

"People are getting bit," Clive said, "Yes, sir."

"Listen," Daniel said, looking at Jen as he spoke, "I want you to take the boats out to the area around Gator Glades. Bring rifles. If you see something that you're pretty sure is a hybrid *or* an invasive, you shoot it."

"Are you sure," Clive asked mildly, "that's ecologically-sound?"

Daniel sighed.

"I'll probably lose my job for it, but this just became an emergency."

"Actually," Jen said, meeting Daniel's eye, "I agree. Such a congested influx of hybrids is an ecological calamity, besides just a basic safety issue."

Daniel nodded. That was no insignificant statement coming from her.

"You heard that?" Daniel said to Clive.

"Got it, Chief," Clive replied. "We're on it."

Jen stared at him meaningfully.

"This," she said, "is not an open-ended endorsement."

"Understood."

Daniel met her eye.

There was still something that he'd been meaning to give her, and a question he'd still never asked.

He reached for his pocket.

But as he did so, his phone rang in his hand.

He frowned – the name flashing on the screen was Anthony Charles Cross – on the second ring, Daniel remembered who that was.

It was Colin Mason's flunky whose car was left abandoned in the Grotto yesterday.

By the third ring, he knew who was calling him on this missing man's phone.

Jen stared back at him expectantly. Daniel tapped the answer button, putting the call on speaker.

"Hey, Ranger," Abigail said. "911 was busy. You said I could call if I needed you."

Daniel glanced at Jen.

"Where are you, Abigail?" he asked.

"Well, it's kind of a long story," she replied, "and this phone's charge is running low. But right now, I'm sitting on the main branch of the Hanging Tree, and I've got about a hundred crocs circling below me."

Daniel shut his eyes, only imagining the connecting dots that could have gotten her there.

The phone's signal faded out briefly. When it came back, Abigail's tone had picked up a note of concern.

"A little *help*, Ranger?"

And with that, the connection broke.

Daniel sighed, looking down at the phone in his hand.

Jen was looking at him steadily.

"You're going out there, aren't you?" she asked.

"I have to," Daniel replied. "I owe her that much. And even if I didn't, it's my job."

He tapped up Clive's number again.

"What's up, Chief?" Clive answered.

"Change of plans," Daniel said. "Send Jacobs and Palmer out in the boats. You get the chopper ready. I'll meet you in twenty minutes."

Then he pulled up the number for Sheriff Barnes' office out in the Wetlands. The line was picked up by what sounded like a nineties-era answering machine, with Barnes' heavy drawl instructing callers to leave a message, or to call 911 in case of an emergency.

Cursing softly, Daniel left a brief summary on Barnes' machine.

Jen was looking at him steadily.

It was time, Daniel decided.

His hand reached into his pocket for the square box that had been in there for weeks.

"I've gotta go," he said. "But before I do, there's something I've been meaning to talk to you about."

And with that, he knelt beside her bed. He took the small box out of his pocket and presented her the ring.

Jen took the box in her hand, looking down.

"How long have you had this?" she asked.

Daniel shrugged.

"About a year-and-a-half. But it's something I wanted to give you since the very first moment I saw you."

Jen looked down at the ring, then at the phone in Daniel's other hand.

"There's something you need to take care of first," she said.

Daniel nodded.

"You think it over," he said as he stood, turning to leave.

Behind him, Jen was sliding out of her bed, grabbing for her clothes.

"Oh no you don't," she said. "I'm coming with you."

"Jen..." Daniel started, but she waved him off impatiently.

"I'm coming," she said, affirmatively. "No way I'm going to let you run off into the swamp alone with that little skank bitch ever again."

She grabbed-up the box with the ring.

"And in the meantime, I'll just hold on to this."

CHAPTER 22

Cross' phone had gone dead in her hand.

Abigail eyeballed the flooded water below. Normally, even during the rainy season, the overhanging branch cleared the water by a good fifteen feet. Today, she estimated not much more than ten feet.

One of the bigger crocs had taken a jump at her, although it was not that fourteen-footer – that guy had retreated, respectful of her rifle.

She didn't think it could reach the tree limb, even at ten feet. Bigger crocs usually couldn't get much more than the base of their tails out of the water in a leap.

On the other hand, the branch she clung to bore healed-over scars, left by big Caesar's jaws.

Never underestimate, Abigail thought.

She kept her rifle ready. Her wrist handicapped her, and she only had four shots left, but she could aim well enough with the barrel propped over her leg, and firing with her left hand.

Daniel was on his way – Abigail had no doubt of that. No matter what drama had blown up between him and his little girlfriend, Daniel would come when she called. She remembered their night together too, and was confident in the spell she cast.

On the other hand, she couldn't exactly say *when* he might be along.

Or what might happen when and after he did.

Abigail had been living off the grid – successfully, until now – for a reason, and if she must be rescued, she wanted a bare-minimum of authorities involved.

The cabin was park department property now, and Abigail had left it in flames.

Of course, the only evidence that she had been there would be hidden security cameras, which were only accessible through Ol' Bill's account.

Or her truck, left on the flooded road just a mile out. Needed to fix that.

There was also that pesky fact of cyberspace.

The phone in her hand, for example – she had deleted the footage she'd taken of Cross, and she herself wasn't in it at all, but it wouldn't be prudent to have it on her person.

And in retrospect, it may have been a mistake to send it on to Mason – foolish bravado against an opponent that couldn't be intimidated.

Of course, she didn't *know* he had also received all the video files on her father's server to go with it.

Mason had mentioned his yacht – probably his mobile central office. Abigail was certain she could access his whole network if she could get aboard.

In the world of tech-voodoo, nothing ever really disappears from cyberspace, but if she could get to it early, that might make a difference.

A lot depended upon how badly the cabin had burned.

And if Colin Mason was still alive.

Abigail tossed Cross' phone into the water.

The small splash attracted the attention of a large croc drifting in below – *moseying*, was how her father always put it – *moseying* on up to you – getting close enough to get a bite.

It was over ten feet, she guessed, and it was one of those with *that look* in its eye.

Abigail shot it behind the skull. In the increasing ambient light, she saw her bullet hit its mark, blowing a hole in the croc's head. The giant reptile thrashed wildly for a few seconds, before rolling over belly-up, and then dropping below the surface.

The other craggy backs hung at a distance, but not too far – it was as if they knew she only had three shots left.

She scoped-out another large individual and shot it as well. It thrashed and rolled defiantly, as if its tiny brain couldn't get the message out fast enough that it had been shot dead.

Then it stretched out and stiffened.

She waited to see if the other crocs would cannibalize the ones she'd shot but, so far, nothing.

Two shots left now. But at least the others now faded back.

Abigail shut her eyes briefly, and was startled at how quickly her body tried to steal a snippet of sleep. She had been on the run, hard-traveling, all night, and she almost immediately began to dream – images of what had happened *before* she ran – images that would never be far off ever again.

She slapped herself awake, her injured wrist providing a painful alarm of its own as she jerked upright.

Abigail glanced down at the water below – it would only take a second's lapse.

The brief wisp of dream had left her in goose-flesh and she shivered.

She wondered if Colin Mason wasn't out there somewhere right now – coming for her, just like Daniel was – a race to see who got there first.

The fire might have gotten him. Abigail had made an effort to trap him inside. On the other hand, she had been on the run, and it had been raining pretty hard.

And she had seen him through the window.

He had been laughing – enjoying it.

Just as he enjoyed *all* of it.

Abigail had a hard time believing he was dead – it couldn't be that easy.

She *hoped* he was. Because if he wasn't, he still *had* to be.

They had established at least that much of their relationship by now.

It would have to happen soon, too.

But first thing was first – she had to stay alive.

Daniel was on his way. Abigail had no doubt. But how long?

Then she heard the sound of a helicopter.

CHAPTER 23

Abigail stood, waving up from the arm of the Hanging Tree, as Clive circled the chopper over the lagoon.

"That's her?" Clive asked approvingly. "She's a pretty one."

Then he caught the glare from Jen and fell quickly silent.

Daniel could see the crocs gathered below. There were dozens, and those were just the ones he could see at the surface.

They couldn't all be from the park – not this many, so far out.

There *was*, however, their staging area back at Ol' Bill's cabin, left full-to-the-brim with hybrid and invasive crocs.

They could have been let out by the storm.

Or someone could have let them out, just like back at Gator Glades.

And here was Abigail sitting on a tree limb, not far away.

He was mortally certain there was nothing she could tell him that he, in any way, wanted to know.

But first they had to get her out of the damned tree.

Clive circled – the Hanging Tree was large and full – lowering a cable from the top meant going through thick leaves and branches.

The chopper had pontoons, but they couldn't get close to the tree with the rotors, and there were *way* too many crocs in the water to attempt to get to her with the little inflatable rubber raft they kept on board.

Daniel opened the side door, shouting down over the drum of the chopper.

"Abigail!" he hollered. "Can you climb?"

"Why?" she hollered back.

"If we lowered a rope through the top of the tree, could you climb up and get it?"

Abigail shook her head, pointing to her wrist.

"It's broken," she shouted.

Daniel turned to Clive.

"Take us over the top of the tree. Get us as close as you can. I'm going to have to go down and get her."

He handed Jen his rifle.

"Here," he said, "if I should happen to fall in, or if any of those crocs get too close, maybe you can take the edge off their appetite."

Jen eyed him back seriously.

"*Don't* fall in," she said.

Clive hovered the chopper thirty-feet above the tree. Daniel attached a harness to the end of the cable, where he hooked his foot as they lowered him into the top branches.

Grabbing hold of a sturdy limb, pulling the cable with him, he began to climb down.

Abigail smiled as he stepped onto the branch beside her.

"Really glad to see you, Ranger," she said.

Daniel nodded to the croc-filled lagoon.

"You know people are going to ask me a lot of questions about this."

Abigail nodded.

"Don't worry," she said. "I'm not going to tell you anything."

Daniel marveled at her.

It took a lot of cheek to say something like that, on the end of a branch, with a broken arm, surrounded by a swamp full of crocodiles – *to* the guy who was there to pull you out of it.

Arrogance or confidence. Daniel supposed there *was* a difference.

After all, here he was.

"Let's just get you out of here," he said, pulling the cable over, grabbing hold of the harness.

As he reached to wrap the straps around her waist, he noticed a new rope had been tied around the branch of the Hanging Tree, right in the same worn spot where that rubber tire-swing had once hung.

This new rope was torn a few feet below the branch. It looked like the tatters were speckled red – like bloodstains.

"You're sure there's nothing you want to tell me?"

Abigail shook her head.

"I don't think so."

Daniel looked up at the chopper, waving them further out, clearing the cable from the branches. Once he got the harness on her, they could pull them both off the end of the limb. They just had to keep the slack tight enough not to dip them in the water as they went.

As the chopper moved into position, Daniel heard a sudden shout from Jen, leaning out the hatch.

"Look out!"

Below them, the lagoon surface suddenly burst, and a fang-tipped geyser shot up out of the water.

The snapping jaws fell well short of the branch, but latched onto the lower tatters of the dangling rope.

Daniel recognized the big fourteen-footer he and Colin had fished out just the day before.

There was a heavy lurch as more than a thousand pounds of croc began to twist on the end of the rope.

Daniel and Abigail both staggered, reaching for the surrounding limbs, grabbing for balance.

Jen leaned out the cabin, Daniel's rifle at her shoulder, firing lefty with the barrel balanced over her bandaged wrist, and cracked off a shot.

The bullet caught the big croc across the plated back – the giant reptile thrashed, letting go of the rope, crashing back underwater with a splash, and vanishing beneath the surface.

Jen took several more shots at other encroaching crocs.

Clive leaned back from the pilot's seat.

"Are you sure that's ecologically-sound?" he asked wryly.

"Shut up, Clive," she replied, keeping the rifle at her shoulder.

Clive grinned.

A moment later, his brains blew out, splattering Jen's face.

Jen blinked, even as the shot rang out from somewhere below, passing right through the chopper's windshield.

Clive fell limp at the controls.

Jen made a jump for the pilot's seat, but the chopper had already dipped into the top branches of the Hanging Tree.

The rotor blades chopped and then broke.

On the outstretched limb below, Abigail and Daniel covered up as the shrapnel was buffeted off by the branches overhead.

The chopper careened and crashed into the lagoon.

Daniel saw Clive's body go flying as the already-cracked front window shattered on impact. As the chopper rolled on the water surface, one pontoon ripped away and the cabin bobbed askew like a buoy. On a normal day, the helicopter's tail-fin might have been touching bottom, but in this morning's flooded lagoon, the wreck floated freely.

It was several long moments before Jen appeared in the cabin, her head popping out the open door, which was now angled up to the trees. She appeared shaken, but managed to climb up on top of the wrecked chopper. She had lost her rifle, and looked warily around at the murky water just a few feet below her feet.

And now, without the concealing roar of the rotor-blades, they could all hear the drone of a boat engine, sitting on idle.

Colin Mason smiled from the seat of his outboard, his own, still-smoking rifle resting comfortably off one shoulder.

CHAPTER 24

The crocs had already found Clive's body.

One of the bigger crocs initially grabbed his floating corpse, and tried to make a run for it, but the others all mobbed him down, grabbing on, tugging and pulling for their share.

That fourteen-footer was still absent – Jen had hit it with a back shot – no way it was fatal, but would have hurt.

So it was likely lurking somewhere below, injured and pissed-off.

Meanwhile, the other crocs tore Clive apart.

"That," Colin Mason said, after an almost respectful moment of silence, "was pretty good."

For a second, he seemed distracted – his rifle hung casually over his shoulder, aimed in no particular direction.

Then he shrugged, turning his attention back to the rest of them, like a man who had almost missed a big sport's play.

"This is all on film anyway," he said, waving his hand around the entire surrounding lagoon. "There's bugs everywhere. Turns out Ol' Bill liked this spot from a lot of angles."

Mason smiled at Abigail.

"You didn't know that, did you, my dear?"

Abigail shut her eyes.

"You might have burned the cabin," Mason said, "but it's all remote. And I already rerouted command of all the functioning security devices to my own system. My home-screen is getting *all* this."

Jen, perched on the wobbly floating chopper, caught the first piece of this, turning her eyes to Abigail.

"*You* burned the cabin?"

Ignoring her, Abigail glanced at Daniel.

"That's not exactly the whole story."

"I thought you weren't going to tell me."

"I'm not."

"Yes," Mason said, answering for her, "there was evidence at the cabin that she didn't want found."

His smile widened at Abigail.

"Old stories and secrets, naked and bare, in plain view," he intoned. "What really happened to Johnny, Virgil, and Pete Marvin. *And* their father."

Mason shook his head.

"Of course, that's not to mention my own poor employee, Mr. Cross. All for simply making a few inquiries."

Mason kept his eye steadily on Abigail.

To her credit, Daniel thought, she stared back – she didn't blink, her own rifle slung across one shoulder. Right now, she was probably gauging how much her broken wrist would compromise her aim.

"By the way, Miss O'Neil," Mason said, "I did like the video you sent me. It's on my list of Favorites."

Abigail blinked.

Mason smiled.

"I'll bet that's a story you thought would never be told," he said. "But as it turns out, you needn't have even gone to the trouble. I would have gotten that show anyway. You were on video all along."

Mason waved to the surrounding lagoon, where Daniel still hadn't spotted any kind of camera – all deliberately hidden.

But he had seen some of those videos himself. And there had been a lot left.

"There are eyes everywhere," Mason said. "And they see what people do when they think no one's looking."

Daniel looked over at Jen, who was hearing many things confirmed for the first time.

Mason was subtle, Daniel thought.

Jen had now just been added to a short list of people Abigail *had* to trust.

And Abigail, not being the most trusting sort, would view that as a threat – which, at the same time, now made Abigail, herself, a threat to both Jen and himself.

Daniel could see how Mason worked – all at once, just by saying out-loud, what everybody already knew, he potentially had all of them divided.

Chessboard smooth.

Mason grinned broadly, letting his hook set. Then he gave it a tug – turning his attention to Daniel.

"And what might *you* have done, Ranger Reid? Back at the cabin. All on candid cameras."

Mason turned a brief eye to Jen, who glared back.

Slice, slice – another division, split right across the sore spot. And just so devilishly deliberate about it too.

Mason turned back to Abigail.

"Not to mention," he said, "what went on between *us*. Last night."

And now he pulled his phone from his pocket. He tapped the screen and video began to play.

They could hear the sound of Abigail's screams.

Abigail stiffened.

Daniel saw it, and his face darkened.

Jen saw his expression and frowned.

Mason leaned back leisurely in his seat, his rifle still hung casually aside.

"And all this right now," he said. "All on high-definition."

He nodded.

"And I have a feeling," he said, "*this* is going to be pretty good."

He raised his rifle, panning the muzzle slowly across the three of them.

Abigail raised her own rifle.

Daniel had his pistol at his side, but Mason's rifle was already on them. Abigail had let go her grip on the overhanging limb to secure her own aim with her broken wrist.

Her aim would be compromised, Daniel knew.

Mason knew it too.

Daniel could see his finger teasing on the trigger. His own hand started to reach for his pistol.

But then Mason's rifle swiveled away towards Jen, standing on the floating chopper.

"I'll say this once, Ranger Reid," Mason said. "Throw away your guns or I'll shoot her right now."

He eyed Daniel meaningfully.

"And reach for that pistol *real* slow," he said.

Daniel snapped open his holster, pulling his pistol out by the butt, and tossed it off into the swamp. It made a small plunk.

There was brief movement below, as the crocs responded to the splash.

Abigail kept her rifle aimed.

Mason smiled. His hand teased on his own trigger.

"Abigail..." Daniel muttered tersely.

She wouldn't do it, he thought. She might not be able to stop Jen from being killed, but she could kill Mason – that would make her safe.

And then the only person she had to trust would be Daniel himself.

Which might not be long.

Then, without a word, Abigail tossed her rifle into the water.

There was another rush of movement from the crocs below.

Daniel looked back at Abigail, who stared resolutely at Mason, avoiding Daniel's eye.

Mason nodded approvingly.

"Interesting," he said. "I didn't think you'd do it."

He glanced at Daniel.

"Looks like someone broke her before I did."

Now he swiveled his gun back towards Daniel himself.

"You know," he said, "I usually delegate this sort of thing. I almost forgot how much fun it is to work hands-on."

Daniel's eyes narrowed.

"Just so you know," he said, "I have notified official law-enforcement."

"You mean Sheriff Barnes? Yes, I know. I have a tap into his phone. I heard his answering machine. Tell me – did you get through to 911?"

Mason laughed.

"I'll take my chances. I heard your message. You didn't even mention me. I'm subject to arrest just being here, anyway. And pretty soon, I'll be long-gone."

"What have you got in mind, Mr. Mason?"

Daniel had done enough reading on Mason's past to expect the worst.

Mason did not disappoint.

"Well," he said, panning his rifle up to Abigail, and then back to Jen, "what I want, Ranger Reid, is for you to choose which one of them dies."

Mason swiveled the rifle barrel back and forth.

"Pick one," he said. "Or I shoot both of them."

Daniel said nothing.

"Just so we're clear," Mason said, "what I mean is that I'll shoot them in the leg, drop them in the water and watch them be torn apart alive."

Daniel glanced back at Abigail, who still kept her eyes on Mason. His eyes turned to Jen, who stared back at him furtively.

"Alright, Mr. Mason," Daniel said, stepping to the end of the Hanging-branch. "I'll choose."

He heard Abigail gasp behind him as he stepped off the branch.

Jen screamed as Daniel dropped ten feet, hitting the water with a splash, and disappearing below the surface.

Craggy backs turned towards the splash.

Abigail leaned over the branch – the murky water below revealed nothing.

But after long moments, Daniel never came up.

Jen's scream had choked off into a strangled whimper, and she buried her face in her hands.

Mason hung on the moment, briefly, waiting for commotion, but there was none – Daniel had disappeared like an antelope snatched from a river bank.

A little disappointed, Mason tsked.

"How noble," he said. "Unfortunately, nobility is dead. And that was not what I asked for."

He brought his rifle back to his shoulder.

"So now," he said, "I guess it's up to you."

Abigail and Jen exchanged glances.

"I want one of you to jump," Mason said. "Or else I shoot both of you."

CHAPTER 25

Daniel clung to the bottom, gripping the roots of the Hanging Tree, counting out the seconds, remaining calm, conserving his air.

He could feel the passage of large shapes – only shadows in the murky water. They were all around him.

A useful thing to know about crocs, however, was that they didn't attack large animals underwater – drowning was their killing mechanism, and if it wasn't a prey-item they could kill with a single snap of their jaws, like a fish, they left it alone. A large shape underwater meant hippo, or another croc – in either case, something they couldn't drown and was capable of fighting back.

As long as Daniel hung beneath the surface, among them, he was just another croc.

He had roughly four minutes to act – the longest he, as an active swimmer, could hold his breath.

Fortunately, the primary congestion of crocs was currently congregating around what was left of Clive – fighting over the last few scraps – on the opposite side of the downed chopper.

No doubt Jen was getting a good look.

He could only guess what Mason had in mind.

Daniel began pulling himself hand-over-hand across the bottom.

Mason's boat was maybe thirty yards out. In the murky water, Daniel's visibility was limited to dark shapes, and light ascending to the surface.

In a clear pool, he could have swum there in a few seconds – but he was forced to pick his way along the bottom, watching for shadows above.

His heart was pounding – he was burning up his air too fast.

Something bumped him in the dark, scraping off his lower leg, the whiplash of a passing tail.

There was a sudden cloud of mud and he realized he had crept right up on a seven-footer, crawling along the bottom just like he was.

But like two fish bumping into each other in a school, the big reptile just turned and skittered off, finding a new spot to rest a few yards away.

Daniel remembered the first time he had seen people swimming with crocodiles on video – a documentary filmed on the Nile Delta. The divers demonstrated how crocs would ignore them underwater, allowing them to swim right up on them with their cameras.

Until the moment they tried to get to the surface.

That signaled they were a prey animal.

Immediately, two large crocs had set upon the two divers.

"I thought it was over for at least one of you," their producer remarked later.

But the quick-thinking cameraman had dropped back below the surface, holding his camera in front of him, facing-off the croc as it approached.

The croc had veered off.

Of course, those divers had the advantage of scuba gear.

Daniel was already realizing his four minutes were evaporating a lot faster than that.

Then he saw the shadow he had been looking for.

Daniel paused for a moment on the bottom, ignoring the demands of his straining lungs, looking up at his target on the surface above.

Just like a croc himself.

He cased his spot – Mason had been sitting to the rear of the boat, facing the tree.

Daniel gathered himself, eyeing the surface.

The death-zone with crocodiles.

For the moment, it *looked* clear.

Which only meant there were dozens of crocs circling in the immediate vicinity, just out of sight.

Daniel launched himself up from the bottom.

He'd seen crocs do this – no reason he couldn't do it too.

Daniel came up over the back of the boat.

He latched one hand on the edge, throwing his other hand over the side, at the same time, gasping a huge breath, sucking oxygen to his starving lungs like a spouting whale.

Jen screamed his name. Abigail remained stoically silent, looking down from her branch.

Daniel latched onto Mason's shoulder, and yanked him backwards out of the boat into the water.

A perfect ambush attack – Caesar himself would have been proud.

Daniel heard a blurted curse from Mason as he was hauled overboard.

Now for the death-roll.

With a fresh breath, Daniel dragged Mason below the surface, twisting on top, forcing him down.

Mason, however, was no helpless antelope, and began to fight back in earnest.

Daniel was startled at the man's strength – it was like wrestling a bear. He also used his single leg to his advantage, twisting nimbly in the water, and landing a vicious kick to the gut – Daniel grunted, losing his air.

Mason also still had his rifle strapped across his shoulder, and now he grabbed it up again, using the metal barrel to butt Daniel away.

Gasping for air, they both thrashed to the surface.

As Mason bobbed up, he already had his rifle aimed – Daniel froze, ready to dive back underwater.

But now the crocs were on them.

Mason turned his rifle and fired as the first set of jaws lunged.

The muffled shot caught the attacking croc in its open mouth, and the big reptile thrashed to one side and disappeared. But there were several moving in. Mason fired again – a second croc thrashed and vanished, but the others were not deterred.

Daniel heard Jen cry out again as he jack-knifed underwater, arrowing for the bottom.

Above him, he saw Mason's kicking legs as the crocs surrounded.

Mason, for his part, had seen Daniel duck under the surface, and with the instinctive intuition of a fast learner, he attempted to follow suit.

But then that big fourteen-footer moved in.

Daniel heard the muffled gunshot underwater and saw the furious bubbles as the shots completely missed, burying into the swamp floor.

There was another shot, and through the murky water, Daniel could see Mason fighting.

Then the big fourteen-footer began to roll. The smaller crocs gave ground as the boss claimed its kill.

Daniel pushed away along the bottom. The crocs had a new distraction.

Still, he was all but blind in the suddenly churning mud of ten-foot scaly bodies rushing past.

He was feeling his way back to the roots of the Hanging Tree, when he came up against the tail-frame of the chopper, drifting just above the bottom.

Hand-over-hand, like the ladder in a pool, Daniel pulled himself up.

Jen screamed as he suddenly popped up beside the floating cabin, gasping. Then her eyes widened and she reached for him.

At the same moment their hands clasped, Daniel felt his leg seized from below.

The sudden jerk nearly hauled Jen in with him. She braced against the overturned cabin, not letting go of his hand.

But it was no contest – whatever had his leg was at least twice his weight. He glanced up at Jen before he let go of her hand.

"Oh no," she began, "don't you *dare*..."

Then he let himself be pulled below.

But instead of struggling, he reached down for his leg, where the tooth-studded trap-jaw had latched-on, feeling the scaly lips, as well as the inch-and-a-half long teeth sunk into his calf, ready to roll, tearing all that tissue loose, breaking the bone, severing tendons, possibly ripping the entire limb off.

Daniel felt along the skull and jammed his fingers into both eyes.

The croc was just beginning its spin, and Daniel dug in hard, riding out the initial torque of the five-hundred pound animal. He felt the tissue of the animal's eyes tear under his gouging finger.

Then he was tossed in the water as the croc released its grip and thrashed away.

His leg now bleeding badly, Daniel kicked back for the surface.

"Daniel!" Jen shouted, as he came up gasping. This time she grabbed him by the jacket cuff, pulling him up beside her onto the wrecked chopper.

He coughed swamp water as she bent to inspect his leg.

"That's going to leave a mark," Daniel managed.

Jen turned to him seriously.

"If you ever do anything like that again," she said, "I *will* kill you myself."

Daniel coughed.

"I love you too," he said.

"How touching," Colin Mason said from behind them.

Mason was back on his boat. He was mauled and bloody, but he still had his rife harging from the strap on his shoulder, and it was aimed right at Jen's heart.

She gaped back, momentarily frozen.

The shot echoed in the flat lagoon like a jaw snap.

Daniel leaped up in front of Jen and the bullet struck him in the back.

Jen gasped as his hands grasped her shoulders.

Then he collapsed.

Jen scrambled, clutching at his jacket to keep him from falling off the chopper back into the water. Suddenly, his two-hundred-and-thirty pounds was dead weight.

Perched on the limb of the Hanging Tree, Abigail stared down, silent as a panther.

Mason laughed.

"Ranger Reid," he said. "You are as stubborn as they get."

Daniel blinked.

He had blacked out for a second. Now he was aware of Jen's face above him, struggling to hold him on top of the cabin. He started to move but became immediately dizzy.

Tears welled in Jen's eyes as she clung to him.

"Don't you dare," she repeated. "Don't you dare."

Colin Mason shook his head sadly.

"If it's any consolation," he said, "neither of you were ever going to make it out of this alive."

Then he turned to Abigail.

"But *you*," he said, "I still haven't made up my mind."

He smiled.

"Last night was great," he said. "And today has been even better."

Abigail glared, her green panther's eyes unblinking.

"I might have to take you home with me," Mason said. "The world just seems a lot more interesting with you in it.

"Besides," he said, smiling, "I need a new pet."

Then he turned back to Daniel and Jen.

He raised his rifle to his shoulder.

"As for you two," he said, "I'm afraid it's time for the highlight reel."

He brought his scope up, bouncing the cross-hairs back and forth between the two of them.

"So, Ranger," he said, "which one of you first? You make the call."

Daniel struggled to sit, to move himself in front of Jen, but she held him down.

Mason smiled, his hand *slowly* squeezing down on the trigger.

This time, however, the gunshot came from behind him.

Mason grunted, blood spurting from his chest, and he toppled forward out of the boat into the water.

He came up sputtering a moment later.

At the mouth of the lagoon, leading out into the main estuaries of the river, Sheriff Barnes was standing in his boat, his rifle at his shoulder.

On either side were half-a-dozen other boats, identifying variously as state police and federal agents.

Mason cried out in pain and inarticulate rage as he struggled in the water. The smaller crocs actually backed off.

But then that fourteen-footer came in again.

Mason went down fighting, but this time, his head was pulled under more definitively. He disappeared with an abrupt splash.

And this time, that big croc simply stayed down and did not surface.

Daniel lasted long enough to see that.

He felt Jen's hands on him.

"We're going to be okay," she whispered. "Hang in there."

Now there were rifle shots as police and federal agents began to pick off the encroaching crocs.

Sheriff Barnes' drawl carried across the water as he led the procession of boats in.

"Looks like your lucky day," he hollered over.

But even as he heard the words, Daniel's eyes began to flutter.

He caught Abigail's eye as she sat perched on her branch.

Unreadable. And she did not blink.

Her eyes were the last thing Daniel saw before everything darkened and the world went away.

CHAPTER 26

Daniel blinked in and out of consciousness as the presiding authorities moved their operation out of the lagoon back to the Wetlands.

There was some perfunctory effort to find Mason's body, but the big croc who grabbed him was holed-up somewhere, no doubt jealously guarding that sizable bit of hard-won meat, which, by Daniel's count, had cost it a running tab of two bullet wounds.

He himself was only sporting one. Although he supposed the croc probably took it better.

The second time he blinked awake, Jen was holding his head in her lap. He started to move, causing them to rock, and he realized they were in a boat. Jen held him steady.

"Stay still," she said. "We're about to get you out of here."

Abigail was sitting on the same boat – Barnes' boat it appeared, although the sheriff had currently boarded one of the larger Federal crafts beside them, and was talking all at once with the varying agencies of officers.

From what Daniel heard, the general consensus was that there were too damn many crocs swimming around the lagoon and they should simply get the hell out.

Abigail looked down at Daniel.

"I didn't let them go," she said. "Mason did that."

"But you burned the place down?" Jen confirmed. "Just to be clear. You did *that* part, right?"

Abigail eyed her.

"It was a place that needed burning," she said. "Leave it at that."

Daniel, for one, wouldn't argue the point.

He blinked out again, and this time when he woke, Jen was looking worried.

Now they were at the main docks back in the Wetlands – somebody had alerted the press – Ashley Wells was waiting in the parking lot at the end of the dock with a van and a camera crew.

Daniel zoned in just as Jen was saying something about not doing another interview with *that* little twit.

Abigail smiled.

"Mason *liked* her," she said. "He said he was going to have her over before he left town."

Abigail shook her head distastefully.

"She's like cotton candy – sugar and air, and not much else. She'd probably give the crocs he fed her to a cavity."

Jen said nothing, but did not disagree.

Daniel groaned, again trying to sit.

Jen gently held him down.

He got enough of a look to see how many other boats crowded the dock besides emergency and media – usually, the Wetlands was sparsely-traveled at best, but today, people were out in boats – some attracted by the police activity, like a car wreck – others were apparently taking the flooding as a holiday – the Wetlands docks were lined with fishing boats, some of them quite high-end.

There was also Ashley Wells, herself – a mini-celebrity, who attracted her own entourage of non-media bystanders.

Daniel's last thought before blacking out again was that he was about to be on the news – a hell of a way to get your fifteen minutes of fame.

When he awoke, there was the sound of a chopper above and the wind-blast of rotor blades.

He was lying on the Wetlands docks now, and Jen was leaning over him.

Abigail stood respectfully back, allowing Jen her territory as she hovered over Daniel like a protective mamma cat.

The paramedics hooked the stretcher to the chopper's cables as Jen leaned over him.

In her hand, was the box he had given her.

Daniel blinked up at her.

"*Yes*," she said. "Just so you know."

She squeezed his hand, and touched her stomach.

"Our kid's parents," she said. "might as well be married."

Jen gave this exactly one second to sink in.

"There, you see?" she said. "That means you don't have the luxury of dying on me."

Daniel squeezed her hand back.

Jen leaned down and hugged him as the paramedics strapped him in.

Over her shoulder, he caught Abigail's eye.

Then the paramedics pulled Jen back and began to crank Daniel's stretcher into the air.

The world began to fade again as they did so.

Below, the two women watched as he was lifted away.

As Daniel drifted away from consciousness, he *knew* he was being lifted upwards.

But it felt like falling.

Then the world again went black.

CHAPTER 27

Jen and Abigail watched Daniel's chopper fly off.

"Congratulations, by the way," Abigail said. "When are you due?"

Jen turned slowly.

Almost involuntarily, she stepped forward and slugged Abigail in the face.

Her right wrist was cracked, so she used her dummy left hand, but it was a good stiff punch. Abigail saw it coming and ducked away, but it still caught her flush.

She staggered back briefly, wiping her bloodied lip with her own bandaged wrist.

Her eyes narrowed, and for a moment, her head leaned forward, like an animal getting ready to fight.

Jen was clenching up again, when Sheriff Barnes spoke up behind them.

"You ladies getting along?" he asked mildly.

Jen and Abigail exchanged glances. On the other side of the dock, Ashley Wells' film crew buzzed to attention, their ears perking like hounds at the brief commotion.

Abigail spat a dismissive mouthful of blood.

"Just been doing a little recognizance on your friend, Mr. Mason," Barnes said. "According to the Feds, he has property all over the globe, but he has no set base, and tends to operate offshore, out of his yacht. He also owns a local island in the Keys. They figure that's where he's got his boat docked."

Abigail nodded.

"He showed up at the cabin in that little outboard," she said. "Looked like a dinghy."

"The Federal guys are looking into the legalities of simply seizing the yacht," Barnes said. "It might be a day or two."

One of the agents approached.

"I'm going to be needing statements from both of you," he said, nodding to both Jen and Abigail.

Jen gave the agent her name, and he turned to Abigail.

"And you, Miss...?"

"Smith," Abigail said, deadpan.

The agent smiled, but wrote the name on his pad.

"Smith. Got it." He gave Abigail a brief once over. "What the hell," he said with a shrug, "*My* name is Smith. I suppose it could be yours too."

Smith eyed Abigail meaningfully.

"Let's hope it is."

He turned to Barnes.

"The roads are still flooded," he said. "We're taking the boats back the way we came in."

Smith started to reach for Abigail's arm, and Lord knows how *that* would have turned out, but Barnes interceded.

"Abigail," he said, stepping deftly between them, "why don't you ride back to town with me?"

Agent Smith shrugged.

"Okay, *Abigail* Smith," he said. "I'll see you back in town."

Abigail said nothing, simply turning obediently to wait in Barnes' boat.

That alone should have been the tip-off.

Barnes had pulled up to the dock first, meeting the emergency chopper with Daniel on board. The other boats had settled in behind. And as they headed back into town, Barnes' boat was last out.

Abigail, of course, disappeared long before that.

Agent Smith was the first one to notice she was gone. Remarkable, because Jen had actually been watching for it herself – declining to sit and wait in the boat *with* her,

Jen had nevertheless been standing on the dock, keeping a wary eye.

Except for Ashley Wells' press-boat clinging on to the end, most of the civilian craft had already left, or been ushered off, before Agent Smith noticed Abigail's absence.

"You just let her walk away?" Smith scolded Barnes. "You didn't restrain her? Didn't cuff her...?"

"Why would I cuff her?" Barnes replied. "She's one of the people we just rescued."

"We have evidence of a crime," Smith said.

"Well, you've got a dead criminal, don't ya?" Barnes answered.

"We don't know that for sure. We haven't found a body yet."

Barnes scoffed.

"And you won't, either," he said. "Not in these waters." He smiled grimly. "That's what urban legends are made of. Swamp legends too."

"Goddammit, Barnes," Smith said, losing patience. "You know I'm going to catch hell for this."

Barnes nodded mildly.

"Well," he said, "you could just not mention it. Tell them you got Colin Mason, and take the medal." He shrugged. "That's what *I'm* gonna do."

Agent Smith sighed, shaking his head, letting it go.

Barnes was the last boat to pull out of the Wetlands.

Jen rode back with him.

"Why did you let her go?" she asked.

Barnes shrugged.

"What would you have had me do? Let them put her in a cage?"

He shook his head.

"Left alone, Abigail mostly minds her own business," he said. "She's like any wild animal. She's only dangerous when you threaten her."

Jen, for her part, wasn't sure that was entirely true.

A lot of animals were dangerous by their very nature.

She had also known animals to hold grudges.

CHAPTER 28

At seven a.m. the following morning, Jen sat on the boardwalk, having coffee at a small diner on the waterfront, overlooking the ocean.

For a wonder, she was sitting there with Ashley Wells, submitting to a second interview – something she'd said she'd never do. But the public needed to know about the suddenly elevated danger. So they sat there, just the two of them, no camera-crew – just Ashley's phone propped up on the table, recording away.

Jen was waiting to find out whether or not Daniel was going to live. The diner was not far from the hospital where she'd spent the night.

Out on the water, off the coast, the boat traffic was heavy – mostly privately-owned boats touring the coast, as the majority of southern Florida was recovering from the storm. There were still areas of wide-scale flooding but the federal units were now on the scene.

And in the general vicinity of Gator Glades, there had been several more croc attacks – none of them had been fatal yet, but that was just a matter of time. All the work of nearly four years had been undone in a day.

Not just undone – made worse than ever – *much* worse.

The just-released crocs, all cresting maturity, in large numbers of both sexes, would be bullish and territorial.

They would also be spreading to *all* the surrounding waterways, especially the smaller ones, retreating from a fight – ten-footers and smaller, working their way upstream into the brackish streams, or out into the ocean and the beaches. And over time, they would *grow*.

There was another incident with a Komodo dragon, this time biting a guy out knocking golf balls into the flooded canal behind his house. His wife had managed to chase off the nine-foot lizard with a five-iron and, once more, it retreated into the canal.

That was two dragon incidents in two days – in both cases it was the large male.

"Gator Glades only had four Komodo monitors," Jen told Ashley Wells. "*They,* at least, are not likely to colonize. Not with those numbers. Although, three of them were female and they *do* lay upwards of a hundred eggs at a clutch."

Buffy made a second appearance as well, this time footage that made the national news, after she was recorded wrapped around a mid-sized alligator.

"What's going to happen to these animals?" Ashley asked.

Jen shook her head.

"We had Gator Glades as a holding-pen. That's basically gone now."

She actually hadn't yet had much time to fully consider this last part. It left the prospects for her own career dubious – how many forty-something herpetologist openings were there at croc parks these days?

Let alone, for someone with connections to Colin Mason.

In the aftermath of the storm, that part of the story was just beginning to break.

That was another part of the reason Jen wanted to give this interview – to get ahead of it.

It was also something to occupy her time while she waited for word on Daniel.

His first surgery had gone well, with the primary concern being to remove the bullet. It turned out he had been lucky – the gun had been waterlogged, and the velocity of the bullet was hampered – it lodged in his chest instead of passing through and blowing out an exit hole the size of a tennis ball.

Still, it got him in the middle of the back – a lung had been punctured. It could have easily been his heart.

Fortunately, Daniel was in good physical shape – most men his age, and their health would have been in question, but he was active and strong.

The doctor that performed the surgery, however, told Jen he wasn't out of the woods yet.

He had, after all, besides being shot also been bitten and mauled by a crocodile – there was tissue damage, possible broken bones, blood loss.

And gosh darn, if there weren't bleeding complications from the tears on the bites – and bacteria, infections, and yada-yada, bullshit-bullshit, we're still waiting to see if he pulls through.

The doctor, a short, balding fellow, rattled off the list, counting on his fingers, as if getting it all straight himself.

Jen had stared back. How many times in her official capacity had she been on scene for one version or another of this riff – the non-promise – the no-false-hope-anything-can-happen speech – not just from doctors, but cops, firemen, paramedics.

Park rangers.

Jen was not official today. For her, it was very personal.

She touched her stomach, and realized she still hadn't told anyone – not her mother, not her sister. The only one who knew was Daniel.

And, of course, Abigail.

As she sat on the boardwalk, having her mostly cordial interview with Ashley Wells, Jen wondered if Abigail was keeping tabs.

Last she heard, Mason's yacht was still unaccounted for. The Feds were pretty sure it was anchored off Mason's island, but his lawyers – still on the payroll whether their boss was alive or dead – were fighting any possible extradition.

Mason himself had suggested anything they might find on board would be as incriminating for Abigail as Mason himself.

Jen was prepared to believe it.

Of course, if they couldn't get their hands on Mason's boat, the only ones left to say so would be her and Daniel.

Jen looked out on the harbor, which was full of boats, some of them quite expensive, and wondered if one of them might belong to Colin Mason.

And she was honest enough to admit to herself that this interview with Ashley Wells also provided the opportunity to allow the specter of Colin Mason to keep certain other things in shadow.

If everyone was already looking at Colin Mason, there was plenty to find.

And no reason at all to look for Abigail O'Neil, unless someone mentioned her name.

Jen was going public with not mentioning her name, casting Mason's shadow over all of it.

And Ashley Wells – 'sensationalist twit', Jen remembered calling her – had pounced right onto it.

"Perhaps," Ashley intoned, glancing down at her camera-phone, now talking to her audience, "maybe it's time to do a story on Colin Mason. A true human monster."

Jen nodded mildly. Now that he was dead, that is, and there would be no blow-back from Mason himself.

"He liked you, by the way," Jen said. "He remembered meeting you back in California."

Ashley Wells blinked.

"From what I understand," Jen continued, "he wanted to make sure and have you over for a *special night* before he left town."

Jen shrugged.

"Use your imagination."

Ashley paled.

Jen smiled, a little meanly – she wondered if that bit would make it on the air.

Abigail would probably like it.

Jen hoped so, because now she, herself, had been added to that short list of people Abigail *had* to trust.

For Abigail's part, Jen had seen her throw her rifle aside, when it could have meant her life and freedom. In the heat of the moment, that had been her choice.

Although, it might be different if Daniel possibly didn't make it.

Or if she perhaps had a little time to think about it.

Time would tell.

CHAPTER 29

Jen's face was squarely in the cross-hairs.

Abigail lay on the top deck of Mason's yacht, stretched out on a lawn-chair, her rifle crooked across her knee.

A twitch of her finger and the back of Jen's head would blow out all over the restaurant wall.

She glanced down to the front deck, where Tammy was playing with Denny. Tammy's new boyfriend, who fancied himself a sailor, was piloting.

Abigail had been busy in the day since she'd seen Daniel last.

Although, these days, it was actually all pretty easy – all it took were a few phone calls – she had means, and a few numbers to go with it.

Once she'd had to do this sort of thing hands-on, but she was learning how to delegate.

Tammy had helped acquire Mason's boat. As she told it, Mason's on-board hands were almost embarrassingly easy to handle, as she and her friends – pole-dancers all – had just walked aboard, by the virtue of their outfits alone.

"And once you get close enough..."

Tammy whipped her knife out of her pocket in a slashing motion across the throat.

The same move where Mason had caught Abigail's own hand like a child. She found herself wondering if Tammy could have gotten her knife in Mason's throat – she had, after all, taught *her*.

Abigail felt quite safe leaving Denny in her hands.

Tammy and Denny had met her at the docks at first light this morning, waiting with Mason's yacht, prepped and ready to sail.

Denny had run to meet her down the dock.

Abigail bent and clutched her son to her breast. They had spent too much time apart in recent months. And might yet still – Colin Mason might be gone, but she never knew what connections might still exist.

She wasn't lying when she told Daniel.

Denny really did have his eyes.

Abigail almost told him at the Grotto – and was still going to, right up until the moment she found out Jen was pregnant herself.

Ironic – before yesterday, she had never intended to tell him at all. She was hardly in need of support.

Now she *wanted* to. But she knew it would just screw up his life. She didn't want that.

This female spider found herself oddly reluctant.

One of the tenants of witchcraft was to beware of the spells you might cast on others, lest it come back on you threefold.

As remarkable as it seemed, she apparently cared.

And frustratingly enough, she found her own alley-cat amorality lacking.

The cross-hairs on her rifle wavered.

Abigail sighed. She knew she could spin it well enough, lay it off on some of Mason's folks – a revenge thing. That would sell to the Feds as easily as Daniel.

And Daniel would be free again – not just free of commitment, but free of the conscience that would have latched him to Jen forever, just as long as she was still out there somewhere.

It would also solve that pesky problem of Jen being someone she *had* to trust.

Abigail didn't like having too many of those.

And right now, Jen was sitting with that little twit reporter – the one Mason was going to make his next highlight reel.

Abigail was watching the pod-cast of the interview, which would be edited for the networks in a later feed.

Jen performed satisfactorily throughout.

Abigail honestly wondered what she would have done had Jen mentioned her name. Her finger remained touching the trigger.

She looked down at Tammy, playing with Denny on the deck.

Abigail put the rifle down. She rubbed her hand begrudgingly over her fat upper lip.

Jen was carrying her son's half-brother – or sister.

That made *them* sisters – whether Jen liked it or not, whether Abigail liked it or not.

Whether Daniel made it or not.

She would keep tabs.

In the meantime, Abigail had Mason's yacht, and access to all his private network – Mason's mobile aquatic virtual brain-stem.

Besides her capacity to systematically eliminate any incriminating evidence involving herself from Mason's accounts, she now had access to quite a few phone numbers.

Access codes, bank accounts. Contacts.

And of course, all his private correspondence – not to mention, personal notes and files.

Mason was gone. He had left behind a global empire.

But nature hated a vacuum.

Who knew what the future might hold?

Abigail smiled, stretching her dancer's figure out in the post-stormy sun, lying back and shutting her eyes.

And in the cabin just below, in the corner of Mason's lounge, his private PC beeped and his monitor screen clicked on.

Receiving messages...

CHAPTER 30

Colin Mason woke on a sandbank, in front of Ol' Bill's cabin.

He blinked awake, first aware of the morning light creeping through the looming trees.

Next, he was aware that his face was in the mud, and that he lacked the strength even to move – to even lift his face out of the filth.

Then he started to cough, puking out water, his muscles jerking alive on their own, immediately cramping, before he finally managed to sit up.

He had a bullet wound exiting the front of his torso, just above the liver, below the rib-cage, passing completely through. When he moved, it felt as if he had the shaft of a spear impaled through his gut.

Mason looked around at the burnt remains of the cabin – the fire had burned inside its walls as the rain had pounded down outside, leaving a gutted-out shell.

Then he looked down for his remaining leg.

It was still there, but appeared broken at the shin, where gnarled tooth marks gouged-out chunks of meat from his calf. The flesh around the bite looked white and dead, like a corpse underwater.

Mason moved his foot experimentally – it definitely hurt, but he at least found it operational. He wiggled his toes in the sand.

As he did so, he saw two eyes pop up not five-feet down the bank, out in the water.

That fourteen-footer had not strayed far.

Its eyes were focused and alert, yet not entirely emotionless – there was an eagerness there.

Like it was happy to see you.

But not in a good way.

Slowly, deliberately, his skewered-gut objecting loudly, Mason sat up into a crouch.

His shin spiked agony, confirming that break.

But he was now looking the big croc face-to-face.

He was ready to fight – like an animal, for his life.

Once before, when a shark had taken his leg, he hadn't seen it coming.

Secretly, he always wanted a second chance to prove himself against one of nature's top predators – a redemption – an unarmed human competing with the beast on its own terms.

Arrogance, perhaps.

But that croc was going to get a fight.

The beady eyes in the water blinked.

And the big croc slid back into the water.

Mason smiled.

Arrogance perhaps.

Absolutely and positively arrogance to think that he had anything to do with a fourteen-foot crocodile withdrawing from its fairly-gotten prey.

That fourteen-footer's retreat had nothing to do with Mason – instead, it was because seventeen-foot Brutus was edging up from behind.

The water erupted in an explosion of teeth – probably the largest, most powerful jaws on the continent – as Brutus grabbed Mason up, snatching him off the bank like a one-legged dog.

To his credit, Mason *did* fight.

For long minutes, there was visible thrashing beneath the surface.

The commotion had already activated the motion-sensors.

From two-dozen angles, surrounding the cabin, cameras recorded it all.

Thirty miles to the east, barely half-a-mile off-shore, the computer aboard Mason's yacht blinked to life.

Mason had added a 'just-in-case' security feature yesterday. The incoming images were automatically sent out to his own personal underground websites – the ones where he had already downloaded the majority of Ol' Bill's videos.

At the moment, they were going into the sites' archives, but without a personal prompt within the next twelve hours, they would be posted for public view.

No doubt the video would go viral, underground or no underground.

Colin Mason starring in his own highlight reel.

He was not, however, going gently into that good night.

The water surface broke, as Mason's head popped-up stubbornly.

Now he was missing his left arm, and his already-wounded leg had been badly mauled – gored by two-inch teeth with a jaw pressure of three tons.

Mason inhaled water, choking briefly – he was rapidly becoming exhausted, his one viable arm struggling to keep his head above the water, thrashing exactly like the wounded animal that he was.

This was always the moment when the victim quit.

That was what made them victims.

It wasn't over until it was over – Mason would fight to the end.

If he could just make it to shore...

He struggled at the surface – the death-zone with crocodiles.

A few yards behind him, Brutus' beady eyes popped back up to the surface.

Mason saw and started swimming faster – a crippled gazelle crossing a river.Nothing more than a morsel in the food-chain, not even worth being fought over.

He struggled towards shore, as the cameras automatically zoomed in, tracking his movement.

Brutus followed, his eager eyes dropping back underwater.

Mason was five-yards from the muddy bank when he was again grabbed from below and pulled abruptly out of sight.

This time there was no visible struggle.

The multiple-angle video playing over the monitor on his yacht showed nothing more – just the flat surface, both croc and prey gone without a ripple.

After several minutes of silence, the cameras' motion-sensors registered no movement and the video-feed ended.

On his yacht, which was currently not thirty miles away, the here-and-now finished downloading on his computer.

It would go public in the next twelve hours, along with everything Mason had from Ol' Bill.

Unless Abigail stumbled on it, of course – it was still very possible she might discover it all and intercept the release.

Or... perhaps let it go out after she deleted her own presence.

That might be more in character.

If she happened to find it.

That remained to be seen.

The fates turned on happenstance.

For the moment, the surveillance-tech on the water had gone to sleep.

In the stillness of the morning, the only eyes that watched were the Everglades' own, and whatever went on out by Ol Bill's Cabin would be purvey to the swamp and the creatures that lived there.

The swamp was always watching.

A thousand eyes never slept.

THE END

Check out other great

Cryptid Novels!

J.H. Moncrieff
RETURN TO DYATLOV PASS

In 1959, nine Russian students set off on a skiing expedition in the Ural Mountains. Their mutilated bodies were discovered weeks later. Their bizarre and unexplained deaths are one of the most enduring true mysteries of our time. Nearly sixty years later, podcast host Nat McPherson ventures into the same mountains with her team, determined to finally solve the mystery of the Dyatlov Pass incident. Her plans are thwarted on the first night, when two trackers from her group are brutally slaughtered. The team's guide, a superstitious man from a neighboring village, blames the killings on yetis, but no one believes him. As members of Nat's team die one by one, she must figure out if there's a murderer in their midst—or something even worse—before history repeats itself and her group becomes another casualty of the infamous Dead Mountain.

Gerry Griffiths
CRYPTID ZOO

As a child, rare and unusual animals, especially cryptid creatures, always fascinated Carter Wilde. Now that he's an eccentric billionaire and runs the largest conglomerate of high-tech companies all over the world, he can finally achieve his wildest dream of building the most incredible theme park ever conceived on the planet... CRYPTID ZOO. Even though there have been apparent problems with the project, Wilde still decides to send some of his marketing employees and their families on a forced vacation to assess the theme park in preparation for Opening Day. Nick Wells and his family are some of those chosen and are about to embark on what will become the most terror-filled weekend of their lives—praying they survive. STEP RIGHT UP AND GET YOUR FREE PASS... TO CRYPTID ZOO

SEVEREDPRESS

🐦 @severedpress
f /severedpress

Check out other great

Cryptid Novels!

Hunter Shea

LOCH NESS REVENGE

Deep in the murky waters of Loch Ness, the creature known as Nessie has returned. Twins Natalie and Austin McQueen watched in horror as their parents were devoured by the world's most infamous lake monster. Two decades later, it's their turn to hunt the legend. But what lurks in the Loch is not what they expected. Nessie is devouring everything in and around the Loch, and it's not alone. Hell has come to the Scottish Highlands. In a fierce battle between man and monster, the world may never be the same. Praise for THEY RISE : "Outrageous, balls to the wall...made me yearn for 3D glasses and a tub of popcorn, extra butter!" – The Eyes of Madness "A fast-paced, gore-heavy splatter fest of sharksploitation." The Werd "A rocket paced horror story. I enjoyed the hell out of this book." Shotgun Logic Reviews

C.G. Mosley

BAKER COUNTY BIGFOOT CHRONICLE

Marie Bledsoe only wants her missing brother Kurt back. She'll stop at nothing to make it happen and, with the help of Kurt's friend Tony, along with Sheriff Ray Cochran, Marie embarks on a terrifying journey deep into the belly of the mysterious Walker Laboratory to find him. However, what she and her companions find lurking in the laboratory basement is beyond comprehension. There are cryptids from the forest being held captive there and something...else. Enjoy this suspenseful tale from the mind of C.G. Mosley, author of Wood Ape. Welcome back to Baker County, a place where monsters do lurk in the night!

Check out other great

Cryptid Novels!

P.K. Hawkins

THE CRYPTID FILES

Fresh out of the academy with top marks, Agent Bradley Tennyson is expecting to have the pick of cases and investigations throughout the country. So he's shocked when instead he is assigned as the new partner to "The Crag," an agent well past his prime. He thinks the assignment is a punishment. It's anything but.Agent George Crag has been doing this job for far longer than most, and he knows what skeletons his bosses have in the closet and where the bodies are buried. He has pretty much free reign to pick his cases, and he knows exactly which one he wants to use to break in his new young partner: the disappearance and murder of a couple of college kids in a remote mountain town.Tennyson doesn't realize it, but Crag is about to introduce him to a world he never believed existed: The Cryptid Files, a world of strange monsters roaming in the night. Because these murders have been going on for a long time, and evidence is mounting that the murderer may just in fact be the legendary Bigfoot.

Gerry Griffiths

DOWN FROM BEAST MOUNTAIN

A beast with a grudge has come down from the mountain to terrorize the townsfolk of Porterville. The once sleepy town is suddenly wide awake. Sheriff Abel McGuire and game warden Grant Tanner frantically investigate one brutal slaying after another as they follow the blood trail they hope will eventually lead to the monstrous killer. But they better hurry and stop the carnage before the census taker has to come out and change the population sign on the edge of town to ZERO.

www.ingramcontent.com/pod-product-compliance
Lightning Source LLC
Chambersburg PA
CBHW061230170626
46809CB00007B/2594